# A Haunted Theft

A LIN COFFIN

COZY MYSTERY

BOOK 4

J.A. WHITING

COPYRIGHT 2016 J.A. WHITING

Cover copyright 2016 Signifer Book Design

Formatting by Signifer Book Design

**Proofreading by Donna Rich**

This book is a work of fiction. Names, characters, places, or incidents are products of the author's imagination or are used fictitiously. Any resemblance to locales, actual events, or persons, living or dead, is entirely coincidental.

All rights reserved.

No part of this publication can be reproduced or transmitted in any form or by any means, electronic or mechanical, without permission in writing from J. A. Whiting.

**To hear about new books and book sales, please sign up for my mailing list at: www.jawhitingbooks.com**

**For my dearest friend, Susan**

June 24, 1956 - March 20, 2016

**Forty-six years together wasn't enough**

A Haunted Theft

# CHAPTER 1

Lin and Viv walked along the brick sidewalks and into the small shop that was clustered with several other stores down near the docks in the island town of Nantucket. Viv's eyes were wide as she stared at the Nantucket Lightship baskets lining the shelves and hanging from the ceiling. The baskets were made of strips of split cane with bottom boards of cherry, maple, and oak and the cane had been woven into baskets of different sizes and shapes, bud vases, wine coolers, trays, and purses.

Viv ran her hand over one of the larger baskets and turned to her cousin. "I can't wait to get started." Her eyes were shining. "Thank you for arranging the class for me."

Lin put her hand on Viv's shoulder. "I know you've been dying to learn about weaving the baskets from this man. I'm glad it worked out."

Viv was a life-long resident of the island and she loved the traditional woven baskets and their history. She and Lin had attended a talk at the historical society by Nathan Long, a master craftsman of the Nantucket Lightship baskets. He had retired from teaching and now only took commissions to weave his beautiful creations, but he was talked into giving a two-day advanced class and when Lin heard about it through the grapevine, she registered her cousin for the course. In conjunction with Nathan Long's brief emergence form retirement to give the class, the historical society was housing an exhibition of Nantucket's baskets alongside some valuable historic baskets that had been donated from museums and private collectors.

A petite dark-haired woman approached the girls. "Are you here for the class?"

Viv smiled and nodded.

The woman gestured to the back room. "The classes are being held in the workshop."

Viv and Lin headed to the rear of the store admiring the baskets on the way.

"I can't believe I got into this class," Viv whispered. The flecks of gold in her chin-length, light brown hair glimmered from the overhead lights. "Nathan Long is world-famous. His classes used to be booked one to two years in advance. He's a master. Your timing was perfect. Thank heavens you called as soon as you heard he was coming out of retirement for this."

"It was all luck." Lin was glad that she'd been able to book the class for her cousin. Viv was a big admirer of the craft and the beautiful woven products. "Just remember, you have to teach me everything you learn." Lin grinned. "Have a nice time."

Lin planned to visit the cultural museum's basket exhibition while Viv was in the class and afterwards they would meet for dinner. Lin stepped out of the store. It was such a beautiful evening that she decided to walk down to the town docks to stroll past the boats and yachts moored in their slips before heading to the exhibit. Tourists meandered along the brick walkways window shopping, heading to dinner, licking ice cream cones, and chatting with family and friends. In a few weeks, the August crowds would thin out and the town would be less crowded.

Lin walked along enjoying the lovely late summer evening and the sights of the many boats with their owners and friends sitting on deck chairs sipping wine and nibbling on appetizers. She was able to catch glimpses into some of the yacht windows where tables were set with china, crystal, and silver and huge vases of colorful flowers were placed around the luxurious dining and living rooms.

Lin smiled to herself imagining what it must be like to be so wealthy as to afford such magnificent vessels along with the staff needed to operate them. Walking by the enormous ships, she had to admit that she was more than happy with her fairly simple life and was grateful to be living on one of the world's most beautiful islands. Lin checked her watch and headed away from the docks through town to the cultural museum.

She was surprised to see so many people going in and coming out and noticed Anton Wilson, an island historian, walking up the stairs to the building. She hurried to catch up with him.

Anton greeted the young woman.

"I didn't realize the popularity of the lightship baskets." Lin walked along beside the man. "I didn't know the exhibition would be such a draw."

Anton looked at Lin, his eyebrows shooting up in amazement that she didn't understand the importance of the baskets. "My dear, Nantucket is known for the design and craftsmanship of these wonderful objects."

"I know all that." Lin didn't want the historian to think she was unaware of the story of the baskets. "I just didn't know that people from off-island had any interest in them."

The two entered the museum which was housed in a nineteenth-century mansion and stood in line to pay for tickets. "This is an important fundraiser for the cultural museum." Anton looked around. "Where is your cousin?"

Lin told him that Viv was taking the class with Nathan Long and how much it meant to her to be able to do so.

"Nathan is a fine craftsman." Anton nodded. "I interviewed him several times for a book I wrote on the basket tradition. He takes the work quite seriously."

"Were you surprised he came out of retirement to give the class?"

"Mr. Long has a strong desire to share his knowledge." Anton gave a shrug. "Even though he's focusing on writing and lecturing now, I'm sure he still feels the need to share his skill with as many people as he can."

Lin and Anton approached the next line of people who were waiting for entrance into the exhibit. The ushers only allowed a certain number into the rooms to keep them from becoming overcrowded in order to enhance people's viewing of the exhibits.

Anton rattled on about the displays in the three rooms of the museum. "I had a hand in designing the layout of the exhibition. I think you'll enjoy it." He lectured Lin about the order of the displays and why they had been arranged as they were. "The first room gives a historical overview of the beginning of the baskets and how the work of the Native American inhabitants of the island, the Wampanoag people, inspired the weaving designs of island settlers and lightship crew members who weaved to pass the time."

The group moved forward and Lin and Anton stepped into the first exhibition room where maps of the island and story boards told the history of the baskets from the time of the Wampanoags to the present day. While they were looking at one of the maps, an odd feeling of alarm washed over Lin and she glanced about the space searching for the source of the discomfort. A pretty blonde woman wearing a skirt and a blazer hurried through the doorway from the next room, her face white. She looked to be in her early to mid-sixties. Lin recognized the woman as a cultural museum worker. The short, slim woman looked shaken. Her shoulders hunched up and her eyes darted about. When she spotted Anton, the woman rushed over and placed her hand on his arm. Lin could see that her fingers were shaking.

"Anton," she whispered.

Anton picked up on the woman's alarm. "What is it, Martha?"

Martha leaned close and spoke into the historian's ear and what she uttered caused Anton's head to snap up and his eyes to go wide.

"The Wampanoag basket?" Anton's voice was high-pitched. He hurried into the next exhibition room with Martha and Lin following behind.

Anton stood in front of a pedestal in the middle of the space, his jaw hanging down. When he turned, his face was pale and his voice shook. "It's gone?"

Lin stared at the empty pedestal and her head started spinning. She blinked several times and sucked in some deep breaths as she experienced a sensation of a cold hand gripping her arm.

Startled, she whirled, but there was no one standing beside her. "What's going on?" she asked Anton.

Martha said, "The basket. It's the one on loan from the Prentiss Museum. It's priceless." She gaped at the pedestal. "It's gone."

It wasn't necessary to hear any other details since the horrified looks on Martha's and Anton's faces told Lin what she needed to know. She stepped forward. "When did you last see it?'

Martha wrung her hands. "I'm not sure. Thirty minutes ago?"

Lin made eye contact with Martha. "Maybe you should call the police."

Martha took off like a rocket to place the call.

Lin looked at Anton. "We should keep people from leaving. Go block the rear exit. Make sure no one leaves that way. Tell people they can only go out through the front. As they come into the lobby, I'll gather them and ask them to stay for a little while so the police can ask questions."

"What if they say they won't stay?" Anton took a few steps towards the back of the building.

"We can't force them, but I'll make notes about anyone who leaves. What they look like, who they're with." Lin started for the lobby. "Anton. How big was the basket?"

Anton gestured with his hands to indicate the size and shape.

"That would be hard to hide. Someone couldn't just put it in a bag or a purse." Lin hurried to the front of the museum.

When guests made their way towards the front door of the exhibition rooms, Lin corralled them and politely explained the situation and asked if they could stay to help out by speaking with the police to offer any observations or insights that could help to recover the historical basket. Most people were happy to stay, but some would not comply and immediately exited the museum when Lin told them that there had been a probable robbery.

The police arrived, secured the exits, and as one officer began questioning the cultural museum's visitors and staff, another officer made a sweep of the premises in case the basket had been hidden somewhere to be retrieved later. It took an hour to question everyone and take statements. The police then met with staff in a conference room to speak privately with everyone who had been working during the apparent robbery of the basket.

When Anton was asked to join the group, he and Lin said goodbye. Before parting ways, Anton moved closer to Lin. "Do you sense anything?" He raised an eyebrow. Anton was aware that Lin could see ghosts. She reported having felt a cold hand on her arm when she and Anton had approached the pedestal with Martha, but the sensation had quickly faded and she didn't know what it might mean.

"Stay aware, Carolin." Anton held her eyes. "You might be able to help."

## A Haunted Theft

Lin nodded and left the building. Darkness had fallen and the old-fashioned streetlights brightened the sidewalks and streets as Lin started off in the direction of the restaurant where she was supposed to meet Viv. Checking the time on her phone, she was relieved to see that she still had thirty minutes before she was to meet her cousin.

Putting her phone in her bag, a cold chill raced over Lin's skin and made her shiver. She stopped in her tracks, her heart pounding, and she slowly turned her head, pretty sure of what she might see.

In the golden light of the streetlamp, a shimmering figure of a young man stood staring at Lin. Dressed in the Native American garb of the Wampanoag tribe, the young man had black hair that fell to his shoulders. His sad, dark eyes pierced Lin's and his gaze filled her with a sense of mourning. Slowly, he raised a hand towards her, palm side up, in a gesture that seemed to be requesting her help.

Just as she was about to speak, the man's body broke into a million glimmering atoms that swirled and disappeared leaving Lin standing alone staring at the now empty spot on the brick sidewalk.

## CHAPTER 2

Lin and Viv sat at a table in the back of the restaurant near the windows that looked out over the dark ocean. Light from the streetlamps and the shop windows sparkled on the harbor water and the lights on some of the tall sailboat masts twinkled like stars that had fallen from the night sky.

"And then I left the exhibition and there he was." Lin's arms were crossed on the tabletop and she leaned forward making eye contact with her cousin.

"He held his hand out to you?" Viv asked.

Lin nodded. "Like he was asking me for help."

"Another ghost. So soon." Viv lifted her glass of wine to her lips. She turned her head to look out of the window. "Who knew there were so many ghosts on Nantucket?"

"I hadn't seen ghosts for nearly twenty years before I moved back here." Lin's forehead creased thinking about the many ghosts that had shown themselves to her since she returned to her island home several months ago.

"They're making up for lost time," Viv sighed.

# A Haunted Theft

The waiter set down their dinners of fishermen's platters that cradled large pink pieces of lobster, white scallops, and baked haddock with buttery seasoned bread crumbs on top. The girls nearly swooned at the sight of the seafood. They picked up their forks and dug in, each one silent as they chewed, savored, and swallowed.

"Delicious," Viv pronounced. Her golden brown hair fell forward over her cheeks as she worked on the meal. "I was starving."

After a few more minutes of enjoying the food, Lin said, "The ghost must have appeared because of the basket. But why?"

Viv ignored the question for a moment. "I've seen pictures of that basket. It's beautiful." She took a sip from her water goblet. "Do you think the basket once belonged to the ghost?"

Lin's blue eyes widened. "I hadn't even thought of that. He must have known that the basket had been stolen."

"He must want you to find it." Viv set her glass down and picked up her fork.

"Why would he care? I can't return a basket to a ghost."

"He *must* care though. It was on loan from the Prentiss Museum, right?" Viv paused and looked across the table. "The ghost must want it returned to the museum." Her eyes brightened. "Maybe he doesn't like the person who stole it."

"How would he know the thief?" Lin cocked her

head.

Viv made a face. "He's a ghost, Lin. Ghosts know stuff." Her lips turned down. "I think."

Sighing, Lin looked out the window at the dark ocean. "After all that's happened recently, you'd think I'd know something more about ghosts. But I don't."

"Well, you know some things." Viv tapped her chin with her index finger. "They don't speak to you. They show up when they want to. They show up when they need your help."

Lin looked at her cousin. "They show up when I'm in danger."

"Sometimes." Viv's face showed slight annoyance. "You've been in danger several times and the ghosts didn't appear."

"Well, sometimes they have." Lin gave a shrug. She had a hard time trying to understand when and why a ghost made an appearance. There had been plenty of times when she wanted to have a ghost materialize and they didn't, and plenty of times when she really hoped one would *not* show him or herself, and lo and behold, there one would be. "Anyway, that's what happened to me this evening. Tell me about your class."

A big grin spread over Viv's face. "It was great. I loved it. We learned some interesting weaving techniques. I need to practice. Nathan Long was really great. He is such a good teacher, explains everything so clearly, demonstrates the patterns, is so patient." Viv nodded thinking about the hours spent in the class. "It made me want to just weave all day long to master the craft."

Lin chuckled. "You can sell the bookstore and then sit around weaving all the time."

"Oh, I'd never want to sell the bookstore." A serious expression settled over Viv's face. "I guess I'll weave in the evenings." She smiled and winked. "Or maybe when I'm at the bookstore."

"How many people took the class with you?" Lin reached for another roll from the basket on the table.

"Only four others. It was deliberately kept small. Mr. Long could spend more time with each of us that way." Viv clasped her hands together. "I still can't believe I was one of the five."

"Nathan Long still makes his home on-island?"

"He does. He lives out by Miacomet." Viv nodded. "He travels frequently though, giving talks on the baskets and their history so he's away a lot of the time." A cloud passed over Viv's face. "Who on Earth would steal the Wampanoag basket?"

Lin was hoping the conversation wouldn't return to the theft at the cultural museum while they were finishing their dinner. The episode gave her such a feeling of sadness and unease that she wanted to avoid talking about it. Lin could feel invisible threads pulling on her, trying to draw her into the case and she wanted to dig in her heels to keep from becoming involved. "That's a very good question." She felt someone approaching and she and Viv turned to see Anton Wilson standing beside their table.

"Anton." Lin's eyes widened with surprise. "How did you know we were here?"

"I didn't." Anton pushed his glasses up to the bridge of his nose. "Can I sit with you?" Anton always seemed full of pent-up energy and it was practically pouring off him as he waited for a response.

"Of course." Lin gestured to one of the empty seats at the table.

Anton sat and reached for Lin's water glass. "Do you mind?"

"Help yourself."

He gulped down half the water in the goblet. "I'm exhausted."

Lin had to suppress a smile. Despite claiming exhaustion, Anton seemed ready to burst with energy. "Were you with the police this whole time?"

"Yes." Anton took a roll from the basket, borrowed Lin's knife and buttered the bread. "How could someone steal that basket?"

"What did the police say?" Viv asked.

"They asked that very question, over and over. They seemed sure that the basket couldn't have been on display before the evening hours started. The officers couldn't see how someone could remove the basket in full view of the visitors. And honestly, neither can I."

"But the staff claim it was on its pedestal?" Viv questioned.

"They do. The police are skeptical that someone could just walk out with it during the exhibition without being noticed. It's too big. It couldn't be tucked under a coat or a jacket or stuffed into a backpack or tote." Anton harrumphed. "How are we supposed to know how someone stole it? The staff says the basket was on display when the evening exhibition hours started. Now the basket is gone, so someone had to have taken it. *How* they were able to remove it with people all around is for the police to determine."

"Do you want something to eat?" Lin had never seen the historian so frazzled and wondered if eating something might help to calm him. "Do you want to order some food?"

"What?" It seemed to take Anton a few seconds to process Lin's question. "No. I'm afraid I'll be sick if I eat anything."

"Are there security cameras in the cultural museum's exhibition rooms?" Viv asked.

"No." Anton practically groaned. "No one there ever thought such a thing was needed and anyway, it's an expense they couldn't afford."

"The police will figure it out." Lin wished she could think of something more comforting to say. She offered the man another roll. Lin wanted to tell Anton about the ghost she'd seen outside the exhibition, but didn't want to add to his worry. She decided to tell him the next day.

The wiry man turned to face Lin. "Did you sense anything when you were at the hall? Did you happen to see any ghosts there?"

Lin's jaw dropped and for a moment, she stared at Anton wondering if he had the ability to read her mind. She shook off the feeling knowing full well that Anton didn't have special powers or skills. "I was going to tell you tomorrow." Lin proceeded to relay the news about seeing the Native American ghost outside the museum when she left the building.

Tiny beads of sweat formed on Anton's forehead. "Oh, my." He glanced across the restaurant for several seconds and then turned to Lin. "You'll need to help, Carolin."

Lin's heart sank. "But it's just a stolen basket," she said lamely. As soon as the words were out of her mouth, the same feeling of sadness that had washed over her when she saw the Wampanoag man rushed through her veins. She knew it wasn't *just* a stolen basket.

Anton cleared his throat. "In addition to the historical importance of the basket, the item is also quite valuable. Not to mention that the basket was borrowed from a another museum and we were responsible for its safety."

Lin had forgotten about the basket being borrowed. Beginning to realize why Anton was so upset, she rubbed at her temple. "Why are you saying *we* are responsible? Were you involved in acquiring the basket from the museum?"

Anton looked over the top of his glasses. "I was." His voice was barely audible. "I am friends with the curator at the Prentiss Museum on the mainland. I made a plea to borrow the basket for the exhibition. My friend was reluctant, but I convinced him." Raising his hands in a gesture of helplessness, Anton shook his head.

Viv narrowed her eyes and looked at Anton. "You said the basket was valuable. How valuable?"

The muscles in the man's face were tight. "Approximately ... a quarter of a million dollars."

Both Lin's and Viv's jaws dropped at the same time.

## CHAPTER 3

Lin pulled some weeds from a flower bed and tossed them in the white bucket next to her. Her little brown dog sprawled in the grass a few yards away snoozing in the sun. The day was sunny and warm, but the humidity had broken and the air was clear and comfortable. Lin's mind had been stewing about the robbery at the exhibition throughout the night and the morning had been spent rehashing everything that had happened while she was at the cultural museum and all that she and Viv and Anton had discussed at the restaurant. After going over everything several times, the three had left feeling dismayed and discouraged. Unable to stop pondering the mess, Lin had tossed and turned all night knowing full well that she was going to be drawn into it.

Lin sat back on the grass and wiped her forehead with her arm. Her dog stretched, lazily wandered over to his owner, put his two front paws against her arm, and reached up with his face and licked her cheek. Lin chuckled and rubbed his neck. "I was hoping not to get involved with this whole thing, Nick, but I guess I'm already in it."

The dog let out a little woof.

There were so many aspects of the robbery pulling her in. She was present in the exhibition rooms when the basket went missing, the Native American ghost seemed to be imploring her to help, and Anton was instrumental in bringing the basket to Nantucket town for display by coaxing his museum curator friend to loan it to them.

Lin made a mental list of things she wanted to do to start the investigation. First, she wanted to talk to the staff members at the cultural museum to see what they knew and saw, and then she wanted to research the antique basket market in case it might shed some light on who would steal the item and how he or she might go about selling it.

"What's wrong with you, Coffin? Sittin' down on the job?"

Lin looked around to see her partner, Leonard, tall, toned, and tanned with streaks of gray at his temples, coming across the lawn. Nicky ran to the man and almost turned inside out wiggling and jumping in delight at Leonard's unexpected arrival.

"I didn't know you were coming by." Lin smiled and stood.

"I thought you'd still be here." Sixty-one-year-old Leonard bent to scratch the dog's ears. "My last client gave me a big box of vegetables from her garden. There's corn on the cob, tomatoes, peppers, all kinds of stuff. Too much for me. Want some?"

"Sure."

Lin, Leonard, and the dog walked to the front of the property. Lin looked through the box in the back of her partner's truck and selected some of the veggies to take home. When she'd gathered them and was about to carry the things to her own pickup truck, Leonard picked out more of the produce and insisted that Lin take those items, too.

She laughed. "I can't eat all of this."

The two hopped up onto the bed and sat sipping from their water bottles.

"How's this thing running?" Leonard referred to Lin's newly acquired used truck.

"Much better than the last one." Lin's old truck was always breaking down and she'd bought this vehicle from the manager of the Mid-Island Cemetery who she'd wrongly suspected to be the perpetrator in a recent case, but who had been cleared of any wrongdoing.

"You heard about the robbery at the cultural museum?" Lin poured some water into her palm and splashed her face.

"Yeah, I heard. That's odd, huh?" Leonard reached down to help the dog up onto the truck bed. "How'd someone get that basket out of the exhibition unseen?"

"That's the big question." Lin gave a sigh. "Along with who did it and why."

## A Haunted Theft

"Well, it's an antique and it's valuable, I suppose, so somebody decided to make off with it."

Lin eyed the man. "Do you know how valuable it is?"

Leonard shrugged. "I didn't hear that part of the story. What could it be worth? A few thousand?"

When Lin told him the basket's value Leonard almost fell off the back of the vehicle. He guffawed. "I don't think anyone needs to spend much time thinking about *why* it was stolen. I think the reason for the theft is fairly obvious."

"But." Lin cocked her head. "Wouldn't it be hard to unload something like that without being caught? Police networks would be aware that it was stolen. Museums and antique dealers wouldn't touch it."

Leonard raised an eyebrow. "Are you sure about that? There are plenty of unscrupulous people who would broker the basket quietly, maybe to a wealthy, private buyer. I doubt it would be hard to sell."

Lin groaned. "I didn't think of that."

"The weird thing is," Leonard scratched his chin, "how did the thief get it out of the exhibition? It sounded like it was a good-sized basket. You can't just pick it up and parade out of the place with it with everyone standing around."

"The staff says it was on the pedestal in one of the rooms when the evening exhibition hours started. When Anton and I were in the first room, a woman ran over to Anton and told him the basket was missing. Who knows how they did it, but somehow the basket was removed."

"Hmm." Leonard pondered how the item might have been removed. "Magic?"

Lin chuckled. "I think there's probably a more mundane answer."

Leonard scratched Nicky's ears. "I'd like to hear what it is."

One side of Lin's mouth turned up and she narrowed her eyes. "You'll have to wait until I figure it out."

They sat quietly sipping from their bottles for a few minutes, when Leonard broke the silence. "Who was the woman who came to tell Anton the basket was missing?"

Lin scrunched up her face in thought. "I don't know if I heard her name. Wait. I think it was Martha." Nodding her head, she said, "That was it. Martha."

"Slender, kind of petite, good-looking, blondish hair, early sixties?" Leonard looked serious. "Probably well-dressed."

"Yeah. That's exactly what she looked like." A question formed on Lin's face. "How did you know?"

"I knew she worked there. Martha Hillman." Leonard drained his bottle of water and slipped down off the truck bed. He lifted the wagging dog down from the truck and put him on the grass.

Leonard's lips were squeezed together tight and a muscle in his jaw twitched. "I don't care for the woman."

Lin pushed off from her seated position, stood next to her partner, and smiled. "I thought you liked everyone," she teased the man.

"Nope." Leonard headed to his own truck with Lin and Nicky following.

"Why don't you like her?" Lin questioned.

"I don't trust her." Leonard got into the cab and leaned out the driver's side window. "Martha Hillman is a bald-faced liar. Take anything she says to you with a grain of salt."

Leonard's comment was so unexpected, that Lin's mouth opened in surprise. "Don't drive away without telling me what you know about her."

"I have to get to an appointment." Leonard's face seemed to have hardened. He shifted the truck into gear. "I'll tell you tomorrow."

Lin scowled, but stepped back from the truck as Leonard started the engine and pulled away. Heading back to finish the client's yard work, Lin's mind was racing again thinking about what could have happened for Leonard to be so adamant that Martha from the cultural museum was a liar.

***

After her last client of the day, Lin stopped at Anton Wilson's house on the way home. She heard

Anton's voice in the backyard so she and Nicky walked around the side of the house to the rear garden where she stopped short when she saw who the historian was speaking with.

Martha Hillman sat at the outdoor table on the deck sipping a cold beverage, listening to Anton ranting as he paced back and forth. Pivoting to pace in the other direction, he saw Lin standing on the lawn. He stopped in mid-sentence and blinked at her. "Are you working here today?" Lin took care of the man's garden needs, doing the lawn mowing, trimming, and planting and tending of the flowers.

"No." Lin shook her head. "I came by to chat." She glanced at Martha and nodded. "I didn't realize you had company."

Nicky dashed to the man's side wagging his little tail and Anton leaned down to give the small creature a pat. "Was there something you wanted to discuss with me?" Anton's dark eyes stared at Lin.

Lin shook her head. "It can wait. I'll come by another time. I should have called first."

Anton remembered his manners and gestured to the woman at the table. "You remember Martha? Martha Hillman. You met her at the exhibition." Anton made eye contact with the woman. "Martha, this is Carolin Coffin."

The woman stood and gave Lin a welcoming smile. "Please, join us."

# A Haunted Theft

Lin started to protest, but Anton interrupted. "We'd like your input."

Lin reluctantly followed Anton to the deck table and sat across from him and Martha. The beautiful woman had dark brown eyes and short stylishly cut blonde hair that framed her face with side swept bangs. She looked like she would be equally comfortable walking a beach or sitting at a conference table leading a board meeting. Something about Martha made Lin feel uncomfortable, but she guessed that her wariness came from Leonard's comment about the woman being a liar rather than anything that Martha was giving off.

"I'm sorry we met in such hurried circumstances." Martha leaned back in her chair. "I understand you've recently moved back to the island and are making it your permanent home."

Lin nodded and explained that her grandfather had left her his house and that she was ready for a change and decided to return to Nantucket. Martha asked many questions about Lin's background, her family, education, and occupations. Lin felt like she was sitting at a job interview and wanted to turn the conversation away from herself and to the robbery.

When Martha paused for a breath, Lin took the opportunity to maneuver the chat to the different topic. "Is there any news about the theft?"

Someone less observant than Lin would have missed it, but something swiftly passed over

Martha's face and the corner of her mouth twitched. She straightened, folded her hands, and rested them on the table. "I'm afraid not. It's a mystery."

Anton spoke up. "Carolin has been instrumental in some recent island mysteries."

Lin gave Anton a look, but he didn't notice. She didn't want him to spill any information about the cases she'd stumbled into over the past couple of months preferring that Martha remain unaware of her involvement. If Martha proved to be a suspect, Lin didn't want the woman to be cautious about what she said or did when Lin was around.

One of Martha's eyebrows went up. "Really? Which cases were those?" The tone of her voice sent a slight chill over Lin's skin.

Anton opened his mouth to reply, but Lin cut him off with a laugh. "Anton is exaggerating. I only ran into someone who was mixed up in some trouble. I had nothing to do with solving anything." Lin gave a shrug trying to brush off the idea that she'd had a hand in determining who was responsible for some recent crimes. "I do find the exhibition robbery mystifying though. Are there any suspects?"

Martha gave a sad shake of her head. "I'm not aware of any."

Lin persisted with her questions. "The basket was large I understand. Are there thoughts about how the basket was removed from the premises?"

# A Haunted Theft

Again, Martha shook her head. "We don't know."

"Was it on display when the evening exhibition hours started?" Lin held Martha's eyes trying to get a feel for the truth behind her answers.

"It was."

"Are you sure?"

With a steely gaze, Martha leveled her eyes at Lin. "Yes."

"Did *you* see it on the pedestal when the evening hours started or did someone tell you it was there?"

A barely perceptible flush of anger rose in Martha's cheeks. "My dear, are you accusing *me* of stealing the basket?" she asked calmly.

Anton spoke. "Oh, my. Of course not. Martha, no one suspects you."

"Well, I hope not." Martha brushed at her bangs and then looked at her watch. "Look at the time. I must get going." She gathered her bag from the deck and stood. "Nice to talk with you." Martha nodded at Lin and then placed her hand on Anton's arm. "Thank you for the cold drink. We'll meet soon to go over things again. Hopefully, the theft will be resolved quickly and our worries will be over." With a wave, the woman left the deck and hurried along the stone walkway to the front of the house.

"Carolin, be more careful with your phrasing of questions. You don't want to make people think you suspect them."

"But what if I do suspect them?"

Anton's eyes widened. "Not Martha." He shook his head vigorously.

Lin leaned her chin on her hand. "Why *not* Martha?"

"Why on earth would you suspect her?" Anton looked aghast.

"Because," Lin said quietly, "she didn't answer my question."

## CHAPTER 4

"And she didn't answer my question." Lin sat in a deck chair next to Viv at the back of John's boat that was moored at its slip in the marina.

"What question?" John came up from below carrying a platter of appetizers with sliced grilled sausages, mini spinach quiches, and small squares of mushroom pizza. He set the plate on the table that stood in the middle of the chairs.

"Martha Hillman didn't answer when I asked her if she actually saw the basket on the pedestal before the evening exhibition hours started or if someone claimed it was there."

John picked up a quiche and popped it in his mouth. "Maybe she didn't hear you ask her the question."

"She heard me alright. She deliberately didn't answer." A slight breeze pushed a lock of Lin's long brown hair into her eyes and she brushed it away. "Why wouldn't she answer? I'm trying not to jump to conclusions about what happened. What are some reasons she wouldn't want to answer me?

Besides being guilty of the theft."

Viv offered a guess. "Maybe Martha's protecting someone."

"If she knows who did it and doesn't speak up, then she's guilty as well." Lin drained her drink.

"There could be another reason to protect someone other than because the person is guilty." John offered the girls more iced tea and lemonade.

Lin's boyfriend, Jeff, came aboard the boat from the docks. He carried a bag of tortilla chips and a bowl of homemade salsa. He greeted the others and gave Lin a kiss and a hug. "What's being discussed?"

They filled Jeff in on Lin's conversation with Martha Hillman.

"Well," Jeff said, "another employee could have shirked their duties and left the basket alone for a while and that's when it got stolen. Martha might be saying that the basket was on the pedestal to protect the employee from losing his job."

"Huh." Lin blinked. "That could be. The employees should be interviewed to try to figure out the relationships between them. Find out which employees are friends, that sort of thing."

"It's also important to find out who *doesn't* get along with each other." Viv reached for a mini pizza square. "Someone could have set up one of the employees to be blamed for the robbery."

Lin groaned. "What a tangled web this could be."

"I think the first thing that needs to be determined is, was the basket there before the exhibition opened or not." Jeff removed the plastic wrap from the salsa bowl.

"But, how to know that for certain?" Viv put a handful of chips on her plate. "No security cameras."

"Interviews with the employees, I guess." Jeff passed the salsa and guacamole to Viv. "The police must be handling that."

Lin kicked her shoes off and wiggled her toes on the sun-warmed wood of the boat deck. "I talked to Leonard about the robbery. I told him that Martha discovered the basket missing. You know what he said to me?" Lin paused for effect. "Leonard said that Martha Hillman is a liar."

Everyone turned to her.

"A liar? Why did he say that?" Viv tilted her head to one side.

"He didn't tell me. He had to get to an appointment. He's going to tell me tomorrow."

"That throws a curveball into the proceedings." John brought some beer and wine up from below. "If you can't trust what Ms. Hillman says, it will complicate the investigation."

Lin thought back on the conversation with the woman. "Martha seemed like she was holding back when she talked to me. First, she asked me a million questions about myself. Then, when she paused for a moment, I jumped in with some questions of my own. She didn't seem to appreciate that I was asking her things. It was subtle, but she gave off an annoyed vibe, like she thought I had a nerve to be questioning her."

"She must have felt threatened?" Jeff asked.

"But I'm no one important," Lin said. "I'm not a member of the police force, not a detective, not an insurance agent trying to find out what happened to the basket. I'm just some young woman showing interest in the theft like anyone in town would do. Why would Martha get persnickety with a regular person who just happened to be present when the basket went missing and who was intrigued by the news reports of the robbery?"

Viv nodded. "Lin's right. It's in the news. There's talk about the missing basket all over town. It's an unusual happening. People are interested and want to talk about it. So, why would Martha resent Lin bringing up the case and being asked some questions?"

"Unless she has something to hide?" John remarked with a raised eyebrow.

Jeff thought of another reason that Martha might be reluctant to talk about the theft. "She could be innocent, but might be afraid that people will suspect her and she wants to deflect attention by avoiding talking about the issue."

"That's a good point." Lin gave a nod, but then doubt bubbled up making her less accepting of Jeff's suggestion. "Something about the way

# A Haunted Theft

Martha talked to me made me uncomfortable though."

Viv licked a bit of salsa off her finger. "Your feeling of discomfort combined with what Leonard said about Martha being a liar makes me very suspicious of her." Sharing a glance with Lin, she added, "The police better keep an eye on Martha Hillman." What Viv really meant was that *Lin* needed to keep an eye on the woman, but she didn't want to voice that aloud in front of the guys since neither one of them knew that Lin had a visit from the Wampanoag ghost and now felt a duty to investigate.

John drained the liquid from his glass and stood up reaching for the appetizer platter. "Let's go take our walk around town." The group had planned to have appetizers and drinks on the boat and then walk around town for a while before ending the evening by getting ice cream. They cleared the tables and put leftovers in John's fridge, and then left the boat as the sun dropped down below the horizon.

The streetlamps flickered on and light poured through the windows of shops and restaurants and pooled in shimmering golden puddles on the brick sidewalks. The chatter of people's conversations filled the air and an occasional burst of laughter punctuated the festive atmosphere as tourists and islanders strolled through town and around the docks.

Lin loved the feeling of warmth that ran through her body when Jeff held her hand as they wandered through the cozy streets with Viv and John. The four chatted about their jobs, the weather, sports, how busy the summer had been, and about a new restaurant that recently opened in town. Viv suggested that they try out the new eatery soon and proposed a much-needed day at the beach for the upcoming weekend. The others heartily agreed with both of Viv's ideas.

John and Jeff went into the ice cream shop to get the treats while the girls sat down on a bench to wait for them.

"Have you seen the Wampanoag ghost again?" Viv kept her voice down.

"No." Lin held the slight hope that she might not see him again. When the ghosts came to her for help, she felt the obligation to do what she could for them, but she always worried that she might fail at what was required to give them peace. "Maybe he won't appear again."

"Doubtful." Viv rolled her eyes at her cousin. "That hasn't happened before has it? The ghosts keep showing up until the issue or whatever is bothering them is resolved."

Lin watched the exit of the ice cream shop to see if Jeff and John were emerging. "I'm not sure how to figure out who stole the basket. I guess I need to talk to the employees who worked at the exhibition. I'm not sure how to approach them in a way that will justify my questions."

Viv perked up. "The exhibition is still going on. I'd love to see it." A glint showed in her eyes. "We could chat up the employees while we take in the exhibit."

A grin formed over Lin's lips as she turned to Viv. "You're a genius, you know."

"Oh, I know," Viv said seriously and then broke into a chuckle. "What would you do without me?"

Lin started to answer when someone who was walking down the street on the opposite sidewalk caught her eye. The man was tall and thin and had a full head of silver-white hair. "Isn't that Nathan Long, the Nantucket basket god?"

Viv followed Lin's gaze and she practically swooned as she stared at the man. "That's him. Oh, how I would love to apprentice with that man. He has an amazing wealth of knowledge and his work is incredible."

"Maybe you can take another class with him."

"*If* he ever offers one again." Viv frowned. "It won't be any time soon."

John and Jeff approached each carrying two ice cream cones. Ice cream drips rolled down the sides of the cones and, taking their treats, the girls licked up the little streams of cream before it could dribble onto their hands.

The four wandered through town enjoying the cool treats as they headed back in the direction of John's boat. The guys walked side by side talking about island real estate and the girls followed a few steps behind.

"John's doing well now." Lin commented on how John was overcoming his anxiety about showing unoccupied homes to prospective clients.

"Yes, thank God." Viv ran her tongue over her ice cream. "He's doing great. I wasn't sure how long it would take for him to handle it." Six weeks ago, John, a successful island Realtor, had found a murdered young man in the bathroom of a house he was showing and since that day, he'd been having difficulty going into empty houses with clients.

When John and Jeff stopped at a small hardware shop to pick up a doorknob that Jeff needed the next day for a customer he was doing some home repairs for, the girls waited outside on the sidewalk. Lin and Viv were making plans about what to bring for lunch when they all went to the beach on Saturday afternoon. As Lin glanced around for a trash receptacle to throw out her ice cream smeared napkin, she stopped short staring down the lane that led to the docks.

Noticing Lin's abrupt halt, Viv stepped over to her cousin. "What's wrong?"

Lin gave a nod of her head in the direction of the cross street. "Look down there, by the first streetlamp."

Viv looked, but couldn't see what Lin was indicating because a small group of people had walked in front of the objects of interest. Viv was about to ask what Lin meant for her to see, when the group moved away revealing Nathan Long engaged in a serious conversation with someone. The tall man leaned forward almost in a menacing posture and his hand poked the air several times to emphasize whatever he was saying.

The girls squinted trying to make out who Long was speaking with. A wave of surprise washed over Lin when she realized who it was.

Lines of concern creased Viv's forehead as Lin turned to her and spat out the words. "Martha Hillman."

## CHAPTER 5

Lin and Viv walked towards the cultural museum for the 10am opening of the exhibit. Viv asked a couple of her employees to stay a little longer at her bookstore-café to cover her absence while she went with her cousin to look at the baskets. Although Viv was eager to see the display, the real reason for the visit was to talk to some of the employees about the night of the theft.

"Hopefully, some of the employees who were here the other night are working this morning." Lin climbed the steps with Viv at her side.

"I can't wait to see the exhibition." Viv had a huge smile on her face.

Lin gave Viv a poke with her elbow. "Remember, you're really here to sleuth."

"Don't worry, I can do both."

The girls stepped into the lobby and paid for their tickets, then entered the first room which held the historical information about the evolution of the baskets. Viv hurried to look at a large timeline hanging on the far wall while Lin moved slowly about the room pretending to view the items. Turning around to head to the next display, Lin bumped shoulders with someone and recognized the young woman as someone who was in the first room the night of the robbery. "Sorry." Lin apologized for knocking into the girl.

The short, slim young woman looked to be in her early twenties. She had long, straight black hair, high cheek bones, and dark eyes. She smiled at Lin and stepped to the corner of the room where she stood watching the visitors. The girl had a name tag that said "Mary Frye" on it and Lin thought she must be working as a guide or exhibit educator. She decided to ask a few questions to get the young woman talking with her. The girl politely walked Lin over to the timeline to answer her question about the Lightship baskets. She explained how the crewman on the lightships took the basics of basket weaving that had been learned from the Wampanoags and then made some changes to the design and construction to suit their own needs. Mary Frye was well-spoken and easy to talk to and Lin was impressed with the girl's extensive historical knowledge of Nantucket and the baskets.

"Do you weave?" Lin asked.

The girl nodded her head and her glossy black hair gleamed under the bright overhead lights. "I learned from my mother. We have some Wampanoag blood in our family. Very distant, but we've learned a good deal about our Native

American heritage. My mother and I share an interest in it."

"You were here the night of the robbery?" Lin questioned. She was sure that she'd seen the girl the night the basket went missing, but wanted to know if the young woman worked in the other exhibition rooms and might have seen something.

A cloud passed over Mary's face as she gave a nod. "I was working that night."

"I was here as well," Lin explained. "It was very upsetting. Did you talk with the police?"

"Yes. They questioned everyone."

"Has any progress been made on finding out what happened to the basket?"

Mary gave a little shrug of her shoulder. "I haven't heard anything."

"What room were you working in that night?"

A flutter of surprise at Lin's question showed in Mary's eyes. "I was here." She hurriedly added, "I didn't see anything. The basket was in the next room." Mary raised her hand and pointed to the doorway leading into the second exhibition space.

"Did any of the other workers see anything?"

"I don't think so." Mary flicked her eyes towards the lobby.

"Who was working in the second room that night?"

"Um. I'm not sure. I work in here because I know a lot of the history." Mary's demeanor changed as she spoke. Her straight posture seemed to sag a little and her gaze shifted down towards the floor and then around the room not making eye contact with Lin as she had before the topic of the theft came up. "The people in the second and third rooms change around. I don't know who was in there the night of the robbery."

Viv came up beside her cousin and spotted Mary's name tag. "Oh, Mary Frye? You're Mary Frye? I've seen some of your baskets for sale in the Grey Lady Shop. Beautiful."

Mary looked relieved and smiled at Viv's compliment. She thanked her for the kind words.

"I can't believe you're so young." Viv shook her head. "I thought you must be older. The quality of your work is special. You have a gift."

Mary's cheeks flushed pink.

"It will take me the rest of my life to reach your skill level." Viv moaned. "And even then, I'll probably never be as good."

"It just takes practice." Mary encouraged Viv.

"You don't give classes by any chance, do you?" Viv stepped closer.

"Well, yes, I do." Mary chuckled. Her cheeks still retained the blush from Viv's praise.

Viv clasped her hands together. "Do you have a website? How can I sign up?"

Mary gave Viv the information and told her when the next class would begin.

"I'm so glad to have run into you." Viv beamed. She glanced over at her cousin and saw the slight scowl that Lin was directing at her. Viv swallowed hard realizing she had shirked her detective work. She collected herself and turned her eyes to Mary. "It was really terrible about the stolen basket. It made me sick when I heard about it." She lowered her voice. "What on earth happened? How could someone steal the basket right out from under everyone's noses?"

Lin moved away quietly hoping that Viv's personality and interest in weaving might cause Mary to be more forthcoming than she'd been when Lin asked about the robbery. Lin edged around the corner and into the next room where she lurked near the first basket on display trying to hear what Mary was saying.

Just as Mary started to speak, a visitor came up to her with a question and Mary excused herself and led the person over to the timeline on the wall.

Viv entered the second room to find Lin.

"I heard." Lin frowned.

"I think she was going to say something about the robbery." Viv looked back over her shoulder. "I don't know. I felt like she was going to tell me something."

"Maybe if you take her class, you'll be able to bring the theft up again." Lin hoped that Mary might open up to Viv since they both shared a love of crafting the baskets.

"The pedestal that held the Wampanoag basket is gone." Lin gestured to where she and Anton had seen the display pedestal. "It was there in the middle of the room."

"No wonder they removed it." Viv led Lin around the space to check out the exhibit. "They don't need to remind the public that a robbery took place here."

Although the girls enjoyed the creations on display, they were intently focused on checking out the spaces trying to get a sense of how someone might have hidden the basket before taking it out or managed to remove it from the room without being noticed. They individually asked the workers questions about the exhibit and then brought up the night of the robbery.

Viv entered the last room and strode up to her cousin. "I have officially struck out."

"Same here." The corners of Lin's mouth turned down. "None of these workers were here the night the basket was removed."

"Time to go?" Viv tilted her head in question.

Lin gave a reluctant shrug and the two headed for the lobby.

"I need the restroom." Viv noticed the sign pointing to the hallway off the entrance area and she and Lin walked in that direction.

They followed the corridor past a few office doors and were almost to the restroom when Lin grabbed Viv's arm and pulled her to a stop. With her thumb, she pointed to one of the office doors. A woman's angry voice could be heard.

"No, I told you already," the voice said. "That's why I fired her. It was better than just threatening her."

Viv's eyes went wide and her mouth opened. Lin shook her head and put her index finger to her lips gesturing the need for quiet. She strained to hear more of the conversation.

"And why are you calling me on this phone? I told you not to use this number."

It was quiet for a few moments and Lin assumed the woman was listening to the person on the other end of the call. When the woman spoke again, her tone was more hushed, but dripped with anger and disgust. "Do something. Just get it off the island before someone finds out." A drawer slammed and footsteps could be heard behind the door.

Lin and Viv scurried down the hallway back to the lobby, rushed out the front door and down the steps to the sidewalk.

"What on earth was that all about?" Viv panted as the two walked briskly away.

Lin linked arms with Viv. "The woman on the phone. You know who it was?"

Viv glanced at Lin with worried eyes. "What? It was? No way."

Lin gave a nod. "It was Martha Hillman."

"Oh." Viv sucked in a breath. "What was she talking about? Was she talking about the stolen basket?"

"It sure seems like it. And," Lin said. "*Who* was

she talking to?"

## CHAPTER 6

Lin was happy to see Leonard's truck parked in front of their newest client's house, a huge antique Colonial set on a large lot close to town. The owner was a woman in her early thirties, just a few years older than Lin, who had been married to her much older husband for about two years before he died and left her his fortune. The house alone was worth several million dollars.

Lin and Nicky jumped out and walked around to the back. Leonard had a wheelbarrow full of rolls of sod and he was busy preparing the ground with a rake. The dog raced across the lawn like a rocket to see one of his favorite people and when he was beside the man, the little creature danced and twirled with joy causing Leonard to laugh out loud. When the crazy greeting was over, the dog sat down so that the tall, strong man could scratch his ears.

"I think that dog actually has a smile on his face." Lin grinned at her sweet brown creature. "He loves you."

Leonard nearly blushed. "Oh, come on." He

tried to be gruff, but his brown eyes were soft as he looked down at the dog and gently patted his head.

The three of them sat on the grass and Lin and Leonard talked about what the client wanted done in the yard and made plans for new flower beds.

Lin turned to her landscaping partner. "So, you were going to tell me something today."

Leonard's jaw tightened and he looked away and stared across the yard to the tree line.

"Well?" Lin leaned forward to try to make eye contact with her partner.

"I shouldn't have said what I did yesterday." Leonard started to get up.

Lin took hold of his arm. "Whoa. Wait a minute."

The man sat back with a sigh.

"You must have a reason for what you said about Martha Hillman." Lin's voice softened. "Tell me."

Leonard swallowed and then blew out a long breath. "It has to do with my wife."

"It has to do with Marguerite? How?" A flutter of unease waffled through Lin's stomach.

"It was a long time ago." There was a faraway look in Leonard's eyes. Nicky got up and walked slowly over to the man where he lay down in his lap. Leonard ran his hand over the dog's fur. "Martha Hillman worked with Marguerite at a non-profit here on the island. Marguerite thought they were friends. Marguerite was the accountant at the place. She was supposed to make a very large deposit and funds transfer that day. Martha told my wife that she thought she saw my truck on the road to 'Sconset and it had been in a terrible accident. Marguerite took off out of the office to go see if it was me. We think Martha stole the money that was supposed to be deposited and tried to pin it on Marguerite."

"That's terrible. What happened?"

"The money was never found. Marguerite got fired. She knew that news traveled fast and that she would never be able to get a job on-island so we talked about moving back to the mainland. She got an interview with a place in Boston. She was so excited about it." Leonard looked up and his eyes met Lin's. "On the way back, to get the ferry home, Marguerite was in the accident that took her life." Tears formed in the man's eyes.

A heaviness settled over Lin and she put her arm around Leonard's shoulders. "I'm so sorry, so sorry," she murmured.

After a few minutes, Leonard collected himself. "The non-profit did an internal investigation that cleared Marguerite, but the money was never recovered."

"You think it was Martha who stole the money?"

"I think Martha wanted Marguerite out of the office for some reason that afternoon so she told her that I might have been in an accident. Marguerite drove all the way to the other side of the island trying to locate the accident. There wasn't one. She drove all around trying to find me."

"How did Martha explain that there wasn't an accident on the road after she'd told your wife there was?"

"Martha just said the accident mustn't have been that bad after all and they must have hauled the truck away before Marguerite got there."

Lin's jaw set in anger and she shook her head.

Leonard rubbed the side of his face. "I don't have any proof that Martha stole the money. Maybe she really did see an accident and thought it was me. I could be falsely accusing her ... just like Marguerite was falsely accused."

"It's quite a coincidence that Martha told Marguerite about an accident that you might have been in on the very day that a large sum of money went missing." Lin made eye contact with her partner. "Isn't it?"

Leonard looked down at the dog in his lap.

"Did you tell the non-profit your suspicions about Martha?"

"Nah." Leonard shrugged. "I didn't have any proof. It was just my feeling that Martha did it."

Lin stared at Leonard's face watching him as he patted the dog. Several times her partner had feelings that Lin was in danger which turned out to be valid and Lin wondered if he had some skill or ability to sense things that he wasn't recognizing or was ignoring. "I think you should pay more attention to your feelings."

Leonard shifted his kind, brown eyes from the dog to Lin. "Maybe." After several minutes of sitting in silence, Leonard sighed. "We better get back to work."

Before they stood, Lin said, "I'm sorry about Marguerite."

"I know you are," Leonard said softly. "Thanks, Coffin."

\*\*\*

Lin wanted to tell Leonard what she and Viv heard Martha Hillman saying when they were at the cultural museum, but she didn't think it was the right time to say anything immediately after he'd told Lin about Marguerite being falsely accused of stealing from the non-profit she'd worked for. After they finished the new client's yard and were packing up the tools and equipment to go on to the next job, Lin started to report to Leonard what she'd heard Martha Hillman saying while on a phone call.

"Viv and I were at the basket exhibition yesterday."

"Again?" Leonard lifted the trimmer into the truck bed.

"Viv hadn't been to see the exhibit yet. I was there with Anton Wilson the night the basket went missing. Viv loves to weave and she loves the Lightship baskets so I went with her."

# A Haunted Theft

"You're not planning on going again? You're not about to ask me to go to the exhibit, are you?" Leonard had a look of mock horror on his face.

Lin guffawed. "No. I know better than to do that." She pushed her tools into the back of the truck. "I want to tell you something that we heard when we were there."

After reporting how they happened to be in the cultural museum hallway, Lin said, "And then we heard a woman speaking in her office. The door was closed. She was obviously on the phone. She said something like, 'I fired her along with threatening her' and then she said, 'get it off the island before someone finds out.'"

Leonard stared at Lin. "You think it was about the stolen basket?"

Taking a deep breath, Lin told him, "It was Martha Hillman saying those things. She's the one who was talking on the phone."

A voice shouted "Hello" so loudly that Lin jumped and Leonard whirled around. Lin nearly fainted when she saw Martha Hillman striding towards them with the owner of the house hurrying along behind her.

"I thought it was you," Martha said to Lin and then nodded at Leonard. "My friend here was just telling me that she recently hired you to manage her yard."

"Hello." The new client, Mrs. Claire Rollins, greeted the two landscapers and turned to Martha.

"They come very highly recommended."

Lin managed to blubber a hello and introduce Leonard. Flustered and worried that Martha may have heard what she was telling Leonard, Lin forgot that Martha and Leonard already knew each other.

"I've known Leonard for years," Martha said curtly. She gave him a fake smile, her eyes remaining flat and expressionless. "You're doing well?"

"Fine." Leonard answered just as tersely.

"I was surprised to hear that you two teamed up together." Martha looked from one to the other.

Lin didn't care for Martha's manner. She seemed condescending and haughty. Lin's nervousness at being surprised by Martha was being slowly replaced with anger and annoyance. "Why were you surprised about that?"

"Well." Martha raised an eyebrow. "Well, Leonard...."

Lin knew Martha was going to say something rude. "Leonard is the best landscaper in Massachusetts. I'm fortunate to be learning from him."

Leonard flicked his eyes to Lin.

"I agree," Mrs. Rollins said. The young woman, slender and petite with bright green eyes and a head full of golden blonde curls, turned to Martha. "My garden has never looked better. It could win a prize." Mrs. Rollins looked from Lin to Leonard. "That's why I told Martha that we should hire you for the cultural museum. There's a garden in the back of the place, did you know? The yard is too much for the employees to handle. We need a gardener." She smiled broadly. "Or two."

"Can you fit in a new client?" Martha asked, her voice lacking enthusiasm.

Leonard and Lin answered at the same time. Lin, wanting to have a reason to hang around at the cultural museum, said, "I think so" and Leonard said, "No." They gave each other pointed looks.

"What sort of work are you looking to have done?" Lin asked.

"The Board of Directors, of which Martha and I are members, thinks that restoring the garden behind the building would be a good investment." Mrs. Rollins smiled sweetly. "An investment in the future. We'd like to hold gardening classes out there and maybe someday, have a little outdoor café to offer tea and coffee and light snacks."

Martha scowled.

"Oh, Martha." Mrs. Rollins noticed the look on her companion's face. "I think it's important to be open to new ideas." The young woman beamed at Lin. "I personally think it's a wonderful idea and that it will add a great deal of value to the museum."

"Is there someone we should contact to talk about the gardening needs?" Lin looked from Mrs. Rollins to Martha. "That way, Leonard and I can determine if we can fit it into our client list."

"Yes." Mrs. Rollins smiled at the prospect of having Lin and Leonard handling the task. "I'll go get a piece of paper and write down the person's name and phone number. Then you can contact him." She bustled back into the house leaving Martha standing uncomfortably with Lin and Leonard.

Leonard turned to fiddle with the tools in the back of the truck and Martha mumbled something about being late for an appointment. The blonde-haired woman rushed off towards her car, got in, and drove away.

"You won't have to deal with her." Lin tried to reassure her partner. "I'll handle the work myself."

"We don't need that place. We have plenty of work and new contracts come in all the time." Leonard pushed things around in the back of the truck.

"I'd like to be able to keep an eye on Martha," Lin admitted. "Working there would give me some access."

Leonard turned to Lin. "Are you trying to figure out the missing basket thing?"

Without making eye contact, Lin rubbed the toe of her work boot in some gravel at the side of the road. "Maybe."

"Why?"

Lin let out a sigh. She couldn't tell Leonard about the Wampanoag ghost. "I was there when it went missing."

# A Haunted Theft

"So? The police will handle it." Leonard had been saying those words to Lin quite frequently, but it never seemed to make a difference. "You don't have a reason to go snooping around."

"Maybe I do." Lin spoke softly.

"I don't like this, Coffin. It could be dangerous. Who knows who's involved in the robbery?" Leonard slammed the truck hatch closed.

Before Lin could reply, Mrs. Rollins trotted over to them with a piece of paper flapping in her hand. "Here you go." She handed the paper to Lin. "He will be very pleased."

Lin took the paper.

Mrs. Rollins chattered on. "He's a very important person on the island. He has many creative interests, loves gardening."

Lin raised an eyebrow wondering who this man might be. Leonard crossed his arms over his chest.

"Thank you so much for considering the job." Mrs. Rollins's unruly blonde curls fell over her forehead. "Everyone thinks so highly of your work."

Lin unfolded the paper in her hand to see the man's name and her eyes widened. "Nathan Long, the basket maker?"

"Indeed. He's the board's chair." Mrs. Rollins started away. "And tell him *I* told you to call. It will be a feather in my cap for securing you." A triumphant smile brightened the woman's face. "Nathan will be very pleased with me."

## CHAPTER 7

Lin stopped at Viv's bookstore after finishing the last client of the day. Nicky rushed to the chair where Queenie, Viv's gray cat, sat presiding over the establishment. The dog leaped into the seat and snuggled next to the feline who adjusted her position closer to the arm of the chair to make room for the brown creature.

The girls sat down at a café table in the back of the store and Lin told her cousin the story Leonard had relayed about the missing money at the non-profit, Martha telling Marguerite that Leonard had been in an accident, and Marguerite getting fired.

Viv was shocked by the tale and responded appropriately with gasps and sighs. Lin went on to tell how Martha was at a new client's house and that the cultural museum is looking to hire a gardener and they want Lin and Leonard to consider the job.

Lin said, "I'm supposed to call the chair of the board of directors."

"Working a job at the museum would give you a

chance to spy on Martha and anyone else who might be up to something." Viv leaned forward with her arms crossed on the table top.

One of Lin's eyebrows went up. "Guess who the chair is."

Viv gave a shake of her head.

"Nathan Long."

"What?" Viv's eyes went wide. "So that's how he knows Martha Hillman. They're on the board together."

"I wonder what that conversation was about when we saw the two of them down at the docks the other evening." Lin rested her chin in the palm of her hand.

"Nathan seemed angry or worked up about something that night." Viv narrowed her eyes. "I hate to say this because I'm such an admirer of the man and his work, but do you think Nathan Long and Martha Hillman know something about the missing basket?"

"The thought crossed my mind." Lin's blues eyes looked across the room as she thought about the possibility. She absent-mindedly slid her finger over her horseshoe necklace. The necklace had once belonged to an ancestor of Lin and Viv. The woman had been able to see ghosts. "What's the motive? Money?"

Viv pushed a strand of her hair behind her ear. "The basket is worth a lot. Money seems the likely motivator."

"Are we overlooking anything? Is there any other reason someone would steal it?"

"We should talk to Anton about the baskets." Viv sat up. "Maybe he knows some history that could shed some light on other reasons someone would steal the basket. It could help to figure out who could have committed the robbery."

"That's a great idea." Lin checked her watch. "Can you get away from the store? We could drive over there now and see if he's home."

"Mallory can hold down the fort. I'll just grab my bag." Viv stood up. "Shall we bring the animals?"

"I'll get them. Anton likes it when they visit."

"Oh, by the way." Viv glanced back over her shoulder. "I signed up for a basket class with Mary Frye, the young woman from the museum."

"Great. I bet you'll enjoy it."

"So will you," Viv said slyly as she started for the café counter. "I signed you up, too."

"Me?" Lin blinked.

"The class is multi-level. Beginners can take it as well. It will give you a chance to talk to Mary. See if you can pry any information out of her."

"I have to weave something?" Lin looked horrified.

Viv shook her head at her cousin and headed to get her bag.

\*\*\*

# A Haunted Theft

When Anton opened the front door of his antique Cape house, Nicky and Queenie bounded inside and ran to the kitchen. Viv carried a plate of treats from her bookstore-café. The three took seats around the large, worn wooden table while the cat and dog snuggled together in an upholstered chair by the kitchen fireplace.

"So you want to know about the Wampanoags and the baskets." Anton poured three cups of tea. "I have written on the subjects, but of course, I am not an expert."

Lin knew that Anton's remark was a complete understatement. Anything that was part of Nantucket's history had been studied extensively by Anton.

Books and folders covered the table top and a laptop was open with papers neatly stacked next to it.

"So," Anton began. He started pacing slowly about the kitchen as if he were at the front of a lecture hall giving a presentation. The historian gave the girls the history of the Wampanoag people and explained about the group that had lived on Nantucket. "There was a population of about several hundred living on the island just before 1763 when an illness wiped out two-thirds of the Wampanoag tribe."

"How awful." Viv put her hand on the side of her face. "What kind of illness?"

"A fever. Previously it was thought to be a

disease like typhus, small pox, scarlet fever, but new research tells us that the cause was more likely to be a louse-borne fever brought to the island by a trading ship. It devastated the people. The group never recovered."

"How sad." Lin glanced down at the books on the table thinking about the Wampanoag ghost that had appeared to her outside of the exhibition the night of the robbery. The ghost hadn't been seen since that evening and Lin wondered if he was gone for good.

Anton continued his lecture describing the baskets of the Wampanoags and how the crews of the lightships picked up the craft and modified it. "As you know, the lightships were boats that acted as lighthouses to warn ships of the island shoals. There was often a crew of six men and during the days, there was very little to do so in order to occupy them, the men learned to make the baskets."

The girls asked questions and Anton answered. Just as Anton's presentation to Lin and Viv was winding down, a knock was heard at the back door of the kitchen and Libby Hartnett walked in. Libby, an older woman with piercing blue eyes and short silver hair, was Lin's distant cousin and she had special powers of her own. The woman took a look at the girls. "Is this meeting about the stolen basket?"

Lin nodded. "We asked Anton to give us some

background information on the basket weaving done on-island and about the Native American tribe that used to live here."

"Did anything he said shed light on what might have happened at the cultural museum?" Libby poured herself a cup of tea and sat down at the table.

"Not yet," said Viv. "But it's all fascinating."

Anton looked as proud as a peacock. "Carolin and Vivian are an attentive audience."

Lin leaned forward and made eye contact with Libby. "Do you sense anything? See anything about the case?"

Libby frowned and stirred sugar into her tea. "I see darkness ... hands, but I can't make out if they are a man's or a woman's. The images are blurred and unfocused." The older woman held Lin's eyes. "The motivation is unclear."

"Money seems the obvious motivator." Viv sipped from her mug.

"The obvious may prove incorrect in this case." Libby clasped her hands around the hot teacup.

"Any sensations about who might be the thief?" Lin stared at the woman hoping to pick up on anything that Libby might know.

"No." Libby shook her head causing her short, silver hair to sway a little around her cheekbones. "But I do feel that the stolen basket is still here on Nantucket."

"That would be odd, wouldn't it?" Lin asked.

"Why not get it to the mainland as quickly as possible? Most people on the mainland wouldn't have heard about the stolen item and there must be a bunch of ways to sell the basket from there. Working from the mainland to find a buyer wouldn't arouse as much suspicion as it would if done from here." Lin looked over at Viv and Anton. "Why wouldn't the thief get the basket off-island as soon as possible?"

"Maybe money isn't what the thief wants." Viv shrugged a shoulder.

"A collector on the island might have purchased it already," Anton surmised. "Perhaps a deal was made even prior to the actual robbery."

"How can we ever find it, if it's been sold off already?" Lin groaned.

"We'll just keep probing. Keep your eyes and ears open." Libby's shoulders dropped. "Someone will slip eventually." She took a deep breath. "What have you learned so far?"

While they sipped from their tea mugs and nibbled on the treats Viv had brought from her store, Lin voiced her suspicions about Martha Hillman and told Libby what Leonard had reported about his wife.

"I heard about that." Libby looked annoyed. "It was never determined where the money went. Unfortunately, Marguerite was let go from her position due to the issue." Libby looked down at her hands. "If Marguerite hadn't lost her job, she wouldn't have been in Boston that day. She wouldn't have been in that car crash. She'd be alive today."

Lin said, "Leonard bears Martha Hillman a grudge, and rightly so." She refilled her mug. "Martha seems to have a grudge against Leonard, too."

"I don't care for that woman." Libby's face muscles tensed and she seemed to be gritting her teeth. "We need to get to the bottom of this. The robbery reflects badly on the island and gives the wrong impression of who we are. The basket exhibition was a celebration of island craft and heritage. Someone marred the joy of that with their evil deed."

The others were quiet not knowing what to say. Nicky and Queenie sat up in the chair and watched Libby from across the room. As if to punctuate Libby's words, Queenie let out a long, deep hiss and the dog growled low in his throat. Everyone turned with surprise to look at the furry creatures.

"Well," Anton blinked. "The animals seem to agree with you, Libby."

Libby's eyes softened and the tension drained from her body as Nicky jumped down, walked across the room, and leaned his head against her leg. She reached down and stroked the dog's soft brown fur. The woman smiled. "With all of us working together, we'll find the person who did this ... and we're going to find that basket, too."

## CHAPTER 8

Lin didn't want to have to find a place to park her truck so she walked into town and headed for the cultural museum to meet Nathan Long to discuss the museum's garden needs. Viv was dying to accompany her cousin to the meeting, but they couldn't figure out how to explain why she was there so she stayed at the bookstore and pouted.

Just as she approached the museum, a handsome, tall, fit older man stepped out from the front door and came down the steps. Dressed in tan chinos and a starched long-sleeved button-down shirt, he noticed Lin and walked over to her. "Carolin Coffin?"

Lin reached out to shake hands with the man. "Call me Lin. It's nice to meet you, Mr. Long."

"Please call me Nathan." He thanked her for coming to see the backyard of the museum and led her around to the rear of the building. Lin's eyebrows shot up when she saw the mess. She wasn't expecting such a neglected yard and garden.

Nathan eyed her. "I hope the condition won't

deter you from considering the job."

Lin's heart sank at the prospect of restoring the yard. The old flower beds were overgrown with weeds and shrubs and bushes grew out of control and seemed to smother some of the spaces. Many of the bricks of the walkway and patio had been pushed up by years of winter frost and Lin had to be careful where she walked so she wouldn't trip. Long vines grew helter skelter over the weedy grass ... what there was of it, and they choked some of the perennials that were making a valiant effort to bloom.

"Well." Lin looked all around.

"It's not hopeless." Nathan made an attempt at encouragement. "Is it?"

Lin chuckled. "No, it's not hopeless. I've dealt with much worse. I'm just surprised by how far-gone it is back here."

"The yard has been an afterthought for years. Money was an issue initially, but the museum has had some generous donations recently and the board thinks it's time to take this space in hand." Nathan walked with Lin around the space. The man bent to pick up some empty beer bottles. "Kids come back here some nights and smoke and drink. We'd like to put a fence around the garden and put up some security lights to discourage teens from hanging out."

Lin could see a spot in the corner where the weeds had been trampled and squashed. Cigarette butts lay in the dirt and there were some charred logs indicating that a fire had been lit there recently. She pointed it out to Nathan.

"That's all we need ... a teens' campfire getting out of control and burning the museum down." He shook his head as they moved to another corner of the yard.

"We thought it would be great to add to and expand the classes and exhibits that we hold." Nathan waved his hand around. "The preliminary plans include setting up tables and chairs in this section here and serving light refreshments. We understand that there can be a good profit margin in such a thing. We could also hold outdoor gardening classes, wreath making classes, plant sales, and teach courses on heirloom plants and seeds. The space is big enough and perhaps one day we could add a greenhouse on this side." Nathan pointed.

Lin thought the ideas were good ones. "It would add another dimension to the museum. I think it would draw in a good number of people."

Nathan Long smiled and looked relieved by Lin's comments. "I'm so glad you agree. Does that mean you'll take the job?"

Lin didn't want to drag Leonard into the work since he would be very uncomfortable running into Martha Hillman. She thought she could hire the couple who often helped out on some jobs if she needed them. "I'd be pretty much handling this myself as my partner is involved in dealing with some of our bigger contracts right now. If you wouldn't mind it taking a bit longer, then I'd be glad to work up some numbers for the project for you to present to the board."

"That would be wonderful." Nathan gestured around the yard. "Shall we walk the space so you can hear what else we'd like done?"

Lin pulled out a large pad of paper to jot notes and to make preliminary sketches. She and Nathan walked from side to side of the garden as he pointed out more of the board's ideas for the garden.

When they had finished, they sat down on wobbly chairs next to a rickety old metal table. Lin placed her pad on the table and showed Nathan what she'd sketched. "These are the notes I took as we strolled around." She pointed to how the patio would be repaired and expanded and discussed some things she thought of adding. "You might think about a water feature here. It would help to create a peaceful atmosphere." Lin looked at the building. "Where would the kitchen be located? It's important to know how that would be accessed and how to lessen the impact of waitstaff bustling back and forth."

Nathan stood and led Lin to a door positioned at the back of the building which led into the above-grade basement. He took out a key and pushed the door open.

A flutter of anxiety pulsed down Lin's back

causing her to hesitate before entering. Sensing her reluctance, Nathan said, "Don't worry. The space is clean and open with windows all around. No rodents or insects allowed."

Lin forced a chuckle and stepped in. Nathan followed behind. A wave of unease washed over Lin and made her head spin. Feeling dizzy and unsteady, she rested a clammy palm against the wall.

Nathan started to speak, but noticed Lin's distress and he turned to her. "Are you okay?"

Lin sucked in a breath and forced a smile. "I'm just a bit dizzy. I have swimmer's ear from being in the ocean." Lin made up a tale to cover her odd behavior. "Some water is trapped behind my eardrum and causes me some dizziness, but it passes quickly."

Nathan nodded accepting the explanation and then he turned around and gestured about the basement space. The walls were whitewashed and the floor was tiled. The room was spacious and clean. "The plan is to turn this into a kitchen. Surprisingly, there's an old dumbwaiter built into the wall between the floors." He pointed to the back of the space. "It's been blocked off for ages. There's a storage closet above it now, but it could be repaired and we could use it to bring food up to the first floor should a function be hosted upstairs in the future."

"How convenient," Lin murmured trying to

figure out why she felt so anxious being in the basement.

"So this is where the kitchen will be to serve the outdoor café." Nathan headed for the door to return to the garden and Lin followed. As she was stepping through the doorway, panic flooded her body and an image flashed in her mind of Viv in terrible distress. Lin's vision sparkled and began to dim. She blinked hard several times and sucked in quick, fast breaths trying to keep her composure.

"That's the tour." Nathan smiled. He turned around and looked at Lin.

"Do you mind if I sit here and make a few more quick sketches?" Feeling weak, Lin hurried to the rusty old table and plopped down in the chair.

"Be my guest. How soon can you have the proposal ready?"

"I can finish it by the end of the week." Lin felt like all the blood was draining out of her head.

"Excellent. I'll show the proposal to the board members and they'll vote. Not to worry, it will be approved. The board knows your work and is aware that your prices are reasonable for the high quality you offer."

Sitting in the fresh air, Lin started to feel better. "I met Martha Hillman the other day. She didn't seem amenable to spending money on the garden project."

Nathan waved his hand in the air. "Don't be concerned about Martha. We only need a majority to approve." The tall man stepped over to the table and shook Lin's hand. "Stay in the yard as long as you need to. It was nice to meet you, Lin. I'll leave you to your work." He nodded and smiled and left the back yard.

Lin sank back against the hard metal of the seat trying to calm herself and she tried to force the anxiety and adrenaline to dissipate. Glancing back to the basement door, she tried to understand what had caused the sensation of danger. She reached in her bag and pulled out her phone to text Viv to ask if she was okay. A reply came in almost immediately. *I'm fine. Why are you asking?*

Lin sent a second text telling her cousin that she was just checking up on her, and then in order to distract her thoughts from the worry she'd felt, she removed her sketch pad and added some details to the preliminary garden plan.

After fifteen minutes of working, Lin realized that the tension had drained away and her muscles were less rigid and tense. Glancing around the space, she made a few more notes and then closed the cover of the sketchbook. The large trees ringing the yard caused long shadows of shade to cover a good portion of the area making it feel like a cool oasis. Lin slipped the sketchbook into her carrying bag and stood up. A whoosh of cold air enveloped her and she froze in position.

Turning slightly, Lin saw the Wampanoag ghost standing under the Beech tree on the far side of the space. He held Lin's eyes with his own and an immense sadness filled Lin's heart before the ghost shimmered and sparkled and disappeared.

## CHAPTER 9

The sun was setting as Lin sat at Viv's deck table with her hands wrapped around a hot cup of tea. Her face was pale and she still felt shaky from her visit to the cultural museum. When Lin arrived at her cousin's house, she was visibly trembling from the chill that had settled over her and Viv ushered her to the deck to sit in the last rays of the day's sun and had wrapped a soft woven blanket around Lin's shoulders. Although Nicky was resting on the deck with Queenie by his side, he kept looking up at his owner checking to be sure that she was okay.

"Then what happened?" Viv had a cup of tea in front of her.

"Then Nathan showed me the basement where they intend to have a kitchen built." Lin raised her blue eyes to her cousin. "I felt weird in there, dizzy, kind of disoriented. I honestly thought I might faint."

Despite her concern about what had happened to Lin, Viv couldn't help but smile. "I wonder if you'd fainted right there in front of him, if Nathan

Long still would have been keen to hire you."

"If I'd fainted, he wouldn't have been able to hire me because I would have died from embarrassment." Lin raised her teacup to her lips and sipped the warm comforting liquid.

"So was it the basement that made you feel tense? Or was it something *in* the basement that upset you? Did Nathan Long say something that produced the anxiety?" Viv studied her cousin's face.

Lin thought it over. "I really don't know. The sensation came on right when I stepped inside. There wasn't anything in the basement. It was just a clean, empty space." Lin shrugged and the blanket slipped off one of her shoulders. "It was a terrible feeling. I wanted to get out of there, but my limbs felt so sluggish like when you're in a dream and you can't make yourself move or run. Something seemed to be pressing down on me." Lin shuddered recalling the sensation.

"When you got back outside, did you feel better right away?"

Lin's heart thudded. "I.... I..."

"What?" Viv tilted her head to one side.

Lin swallowed hard. Even though she didn't want to alarm Viv by telling her of the horrible feeling she'd had that her cousin was in danger, Lin couldn't hide the fact from her cousin so she blurted it out. "I had the awful sensation that you were hurt or in peril."

Viv looked like she'd been slapped. "Me? In danger? That was your feeling?" Viv's cheeks lost their rosy glow. "That's why you texted me asking if I was okay."

Lin nodded, her eyes wide with worry. "It probably doesn't mean anything. I was probably feeling anxious and for some reason I fixated on you."

Viv leveled her gaze across the table at Lin. "You probably felt it because it was a premonition." Pushing her hair behind her ear, she glanced over her shoulders at her darkening backyard. "Should we go inside?"

"I think we're safe." Lin looked out over the yard just to be sure.

"For now." Viv's voice trembled. "What does it mean? What's going to happen to me?"

"Nothing." Lin set her jaw. "Nothing's going to happen to you. It was just a silly feeling. For some reason, I felt panicky and projected it onto you."

"Don't do that anymore, okay?" Viv took a swallow of her tea. "Project it onto someone else."

"In the meantime...."

"I know." Viv rubbed her forehead. "I'll be careful."

"There's something else." Lin folded her arms onto the table.

Viv let out a groan.

"I saw the Wampanoag ghost again, in the garden behind the cultural museum."

"He came back?" Viv leaned forward.

"He looked at me." Lin turned her eyes to the tall trees that ringed Viv's yard. "And his look filled me with sadness."

The girls sat quietly for a few minutes and then Viv said, "Let's talk about the case. Let's be proactive and not just sit here worrying and fretting."

The corners of Lin's mouth turned up. She loved how Viv could focus on figuring things out even when worry was about to consume her. Lin ran her index finger over her horseshoe necklace. "That's a good idea. Let's talk about suspects. The ghost has only shown himself twice and both times were outside the cultural museum. Do you think that the ghost appears there because the thief is connected in some way to the museum?"

"It could be." Viv checked the time on her phone to see if the shepherd's pie needed to come out of the oven. "Then there's Martha Hillman. There are a lot of reasons to suspect her."

"What about Nathan Long?"

"Nathan? No." Viv gave a hard shake of her head. "Impossible. He's a nice man. He wouldn't steal the basket."

"He could be hiding behind the nice-man façade. He's so wonderful no one would ever think he could have done it. It's the perfect front." Lin went on when she saw the skeptical look wash over Viv. "Nathan has access to the rooms at the museum.

He can wander wherever he wants to go and no one would think anything of it. I bet he could think of a way to get that basket out there without being noticed."

Viv narrowed her eyes. "If he could think of a way to get the basket out of the cultural museum, then he might be helping the police figure out how the robber escaped with it. And anyway, why would he do it?"

"The money?" Lin cocked her head.

"What would the money get him that he doesn't already have? He must be wealthy. He is a respected craftsman, he's in huge demand to teach and to speak. He must make plenty of money. He has what money can't buy, the respect and esteem of others. Why would he risk that?"

"Maybe he just wants that antique basket. It's really one of a kind." Lin pulled the blanket up around her shoulders and lifted an edge up over her head like a hood. "Like you said, he has everything. He loves the baskets. So maybe he wants the one thing he doesn't have … the antique basket."

Viv scrunched up her forehead. She realized that Lin's idea was plausible. "It makes me sad to think he would do such a thing." A long sigh slipped from her throat. "Who else is a possible suspect?"

"Mary Frye?" Lin asked.

"Oh! That reminds me." Viv straightened. "We need to eat. We need to get going. We have the class in less than an hour."

Lin looked puzzled.

"Mary Frye's class. We're going to it. It's tonight."

An expression of horror formed on Lin's face. "Tonight? Can we skip it?"

Viv shook her head. "We're going." She stood up to head to the kitchen to get the meal out of the oven. "If you think Mary might be a suspect, then this will give you a chance to question her."

"Like you said before, I think she wanted to tell us something when we saw her at the exhibition."

"So while you're weaving the reeds, you can try and coax her to spill what she knows. If anything."

"I'm not crafty," Lin moaned. "I'm going to look like a fool."

"You might want to modify that statement." With a grin, Viv stared at her cousin wrapped up tightly in the blanket with only her pale face sticking out from under the fabric. "I think you've already achieved the look."

***

Lin sat at the end of the long wooden table struggling with trying to weave the cane reeds the way Mary Frye had told her to interlace them. Viv sat across from her chatting amiably with two other women who were working the strips of cane into intricately woven baskets. After one glance at what the others were doing, Lin made sure not to look at their creations again because it would have caused her to run from the old barn in shame.

"That's going well." Mary Frye leaned down to watch Lin moving the cane between her fingers. "You've improved already." The lovely young woman smiled at Lin and sat down next to her to give more pointers and suggestions.

"I'm not very good at this sort of thing." Lin slid the reed under the first one.

"Nonsense. Anyone can master the weaving."

"Are you attending college?" Lin wanted to ask questions to divert Mary's attention from her fumbling fingers and to get a sense of her and what she might know about the robbery of the antique basket.

"I'm working on a master's degree. I'm studying art history. In the summer, I come back to the island to teach classes and make baskets with my mother. She sells them in her shop in town. And of course, I work in the town museum, too." Her long dark hair fell forward over her shoulder when she leaned down to help Lin adjust her technique.

"What shop does your mother own?"

"It's a couple of blocks from the boat docks. Just a small place. It's called Oak, Ash, and Hickory."

For a few minutes, Lin chatted with Mary about different things and then asked, "Were you only in the front room of the cultural museum when the basket went missing?"

## A Haunted Theft

"I was working in the first room like always. Right where we met the day you came with your cousin to the exhibit."

"Was the basket on the pedestal when the evening hours began?" Lin knew she'd asked Mary these same questions before, but wanted to see if she would answer them in the same way.

"I don't know. When I came to work, I entered through the lobby and took my position in the first room."

"Do all the employees come in the same way?"

"You mean through the front door?"

Lin nodded. "Are any other doors open besides the front? Can employees enter from any other doors?"

"There's a code on the back door. We can go in through that door as well as through the front, but visitors can only enter through the main entrance."

"All the employees get the code? That seems like a breach. Can't you all just enter any time of the day or night? You punch in the code and you can go in?"

"Only during business hours." Mary pointed to the spot on the small basket where Lin should lace the reed. "At the end of the evening, the curator, or whoever is in charge, disables the door code for the night. It won't allow access until its reactivated the next morning when someone comes to open up."

"Is it possible that the curator forgot to disable the code and that's how the basket was stolen?" Lin looked at Mary.

"But the basket was on the pedestal during the daytime exhibition hours. It was only noticed to be missing when the evening hours started."

"Couldn't someone have used the code to come in the back door during the dinner hour when the museum was closed?" Lin wiped her hand on her jeans.

"The code only works during the times when the museum is open. It would have been disabled during the dinner hour when the building is closed to the public."

"Were the police told about the back door?"

"I'm just a part-time worker. I don't know what anyone told the police."

Lin spent a few minutes paying attention to her weaving while her mind raced. Someone could have forgotten to disarm the code. The door was unlocked. Anyone could have gone inside and left with the basket. She paused and shifted slightly on the bench to make eye contact with Mary. "Did you know the person who got let go from the cultural museum?"

Mary sat straighter and her eyes widened. A flicker of something passed over her face and was gone. She seemed surprised that Lin asked the question. "Who?"

"I heard someone got fired. I wondered if you knew the person."

"I don't think so." Mary stood up abruptly. "I'm

going to check on the others."

Watching the young woman out of the corner of her eye, Lin had the distinct impression that Mary was hiding something.

## CHAPTER 10

Lin and Viv had lunch on John's boat and then headed a few blocks to a side street tucked off the main section of town.

"I can't believe I've never been to this shop." Viv smiled. "I can't wait to go in."

"Remember why we're here though." Lin spotted the small shop tucked between a gift shop and a clothing boutique. "Keep your eyes and ears open."

The girls entered the tiny, cozy store. Nantucket baskets and trays and purses lined shelves and hung from the low ceiling. The golden wood floor nearly sparkled in the sunlight. An older woman with a long gray braid curling over her shoulder sat hunched at a table in one corner of the place. Lin was surprised that this woman was Mary's mother. She looked so much older than Lin expected.

Despite the woman's arthritic knuckles, the fingers of her hands moved skillfully weaving the reeds into an oval basket. Viv watched from across the room as the woman performed her craft.

## A Haunted Theft

Without lifting her head, the woman spoke. "You can come closer."

Viv smiled and moved over to the table.

"Do you work the baskets?" The woman lifted her eyes to Viv for just a second and then returned her attention to her work.

"I do." Viv watched the woman weave. "I'm always trying to learn."

"So am I." A grin lifted the corners of the older woman's mouth. "There is always something new to discover from the wood."

Lin walked over and stood next to her cousin.

The woman's gnarled hands stopped moving the strips of ash and looked up at Lin. She blinked several times. Her eyes seemed to bore into Lin and for a moment, Lin felt like the woman could see right through her.

"Are you sisters?"

Lin wondered what the woman could sense about them. The two cousins didn't look alike until you got to know them and then, a resemblance might be noted, but it wasn't really a physical sameness that the girls shared. Lin had long brown hair, was taller then her cousin, and her physique was slim and fit. Viv had chin-length light brown hair with golden highlights. She carried a few extra pounds and was shorter. They both had the same blazing, bright blue eyes though.

Lin shook her head.

"But you're like sisters, aren't you?" The woman

cocked her head still studying the two young women before her.

Viv smiled. "We're cousins."

"What are your names?"

"I'm Vivian Coffin and this is my cousin, Carolin Coffin."

Lin spoke up. "Everyone calls me Lin."

"I'm Lacey Frye." The woman gave a nod that was very much like a slight bow. "What brings you in today?"

"I love the baskets and I've never been in here before, even though I've lived on the island my whole life." Viv chatted amiably. "I can't understand why I never came by. Your place is sort of tucked away, I guess."

"My hours are often limited." Lacey gave a sigh and a shrug. "I have some health problems. I don't have the stamina I once had. But, I love what I do and I need to keep busy."

"We're like that, too. We like to be busy." Viv nodded to her cousin. "We both run businesses." The conversation went on for a while as Viv told Lacey about the bookstore-café, her band and the gigs they performed, and how Lin worked part-time as a computer programmer and also ran a full-time landscaping business.

Lin eyed Lacey to gauge her interest in Viv's monologue and was relieved to see that she was enjoying the chat.

Viv went on. "Lin is about to get a new contract

to do the landscaping at the cultural museum."

"Well, maybe." Lin gave a little shrug. "We'll see how the proposal is received."

Lacey gave Lin a look that was hard to decipher. "Who invited you to bid on the job?"

"One of the board members is a client of mine. She asked me if I'd be interested in the work and told me to contact someone about it."

"Who was the board member who asked if you'd be interested in the job?" Lacey asked.

"Claire Rollins."

Lacey narrowed her eyes. "Who did she tell you to speak with?"

"Nathan Long."

"I see." A strange look flickered over the woman's face.

"Do you know Mr. Long?" Lin asked.

"I know him." The words sounded icy and brittle.

"Have you worked with Nathan?" Viv seemed oblivious to the tone in Lacey's voice. "I took a class with him recently."

"I worked with Nathan a long time ago. He's made a quite a name for himself, hasn't he?"

Lin couldn't put a finger on the emotion that was emanating from Lacey. Someone might think it was jealousy over Nathan's successful career and notoriety, but Lin was sure that wasn't the reason. It seemed to be something else. She concentrated trying to understand the currents that were floating on the air. Was it anger? Regret? Sadness? Lin had almost grasped the feeling when the sensation seemed to break apart and slip away.

Viv's voice brought Lin out of her focused state. "I've been learning to make the baskets for a few years. I don't have a lot of time to devote to it, but maybe someday." Viv pulled up a chair to Lacey's table. "May I sit and watch you work for a little while?"

"That would be very nice." Lacey picked up a splint of ash and started to weave.

Lin stood by the table. "We met your daughter. Mary."

"Did you? At the museum?" Lacey bent over her work. "Or at the breakfast shop?"

"At the museum," Lin replied. "We didn't know she worked at a breakfast place."

"Mary works at the shop over on Newcomb Street. She's as busy as a bee, that girl. It's nice to have her on-island in the summers. She works with me some evenings and we weave together."

"We took a class with her last night out at her friend's place." Viv leaned forward to watch Lacey as she fiddled with a piece of the wood.

"Mary's a good teacher." Lacey nodded.

Lin decided that now would be a good time to bring up the stolen basket. "I was at the cultural museum the night they discovered that the antique basket was missing."

"Were you?" Lacey slowly raised her face to

make eye contact with Lin. "Did you notice anything amiss when you were there?"

"Not really. We'd only just arrived when one of the workers rushed over to the man I was with to tell him the basket was missing."

"Who were you with?"

"Anton Wilson, a local historian."

"I know who he is." Lacey gave a nod. Her expression seemed to imply a favorable impression of Anton. The woman's brown eyes narrowed. "Who reported the issue to Anton?"

"Martha Hillman."

A scowl pulled Lacey's facial muscles down.

"Do you know her?" Lin hoped to get Lacey to say something about Martha.

"I know her," Lacey said, her voice was tight. "She shouldn't have that job."

"No?" Lin cocked her head.

Lacey ignored Lin's question. "What room were you in when they noticed the missing object?"

"The first exhibition room. Your daughter was in that room as well."

"What did Martha say to Anton?"

Lin thought that Lacey would make a great detective. "She whispered, so I couldn't hear what she said, but Anton blurted out a question. Well, it was more like an exclamation about the basket being missing. We hurried into the next room and the pedestal was empty. I suggested that Martha call the police right away."

Lacey seemed to be pondering the information.

Lin said, "Your daughter told me that the employees use the rear entrance during working hours to enter the museum. It's a staff entrance, I guess. It seems it might be easy enough for someone to come in that way and make off with the basket. I'm sure the police must think the same thing."

"Yes." Lacey's brow furrowed. "That door should have been locked when such a valuable piece as the basket was present in the museum. They'll never be able to acquire something like that again. It won't happen if the sending institution feels security in the museum is lax."

Viv had been listening to the conversation, but now asked a question. She looked at Lacey. "Why do you think it was stolen? To sell it and get the money?"

Lacey put her materials down and wiped her hand on a small towel. "I'm sure the police think the basket was stolen for the money which has them running down the wrong path and barking up an imaginary tree."

The door to the shop opened and three women entered and began admiring the baskets on the store shelves.

"You don't think it was taken to sell it off?" Lin kept her voice soft.

The older woman's face clouded. "I do not." When one of the customers asked her a question,

Lacey rose from her seat and crossed the space to where the customers stood looking over a large woven tray. "Nice talking with you girls."

As Lin and Viv left the shop, a cold breeze blew over Lin's skin and she shuddered. "Wow, the ocean breeze must have changed direction. It's really cold."

"You're cold?" Viv was surprised that her cousin felt cold in the heat of the day. She stopped short and turned to Lin. "*I'm* not cold. It isn't cold out."

"Oh." Lin took in a breath and then shifted her gaze across the cobblestone street.

On the opposite sidewalk, dressed in eighteenth-century garments, the ghost of Lin's ancestor, Sebastian Coffin, stood glimmering in the sunlight.

## CHAPTER 11

"Who is it?" Viv gripped her cousin's arm. "Where is it?" Even though she couldn't see ghosts, her head moved from side to side scanning the area.

Lin made eye contact with the ghost of her ancestor. "It's Sebastian," she whispered. "He's standing across the street."

"Thank heavens he's on *that* side of the road." Viv's grip on Lin's arm loosened a bit. "Tell him to stay over there."

"He won't come closer if you're with me." Lin closed her eyes for a second trying to clear her mind in the hopes the ghost would send her a mental message. She tried to relax her muscles and calm her thoughts, but her brain was jumping from thing to thing trying to determine the reason for Sebastian's appearance.

Lin sighed and opened her eyes. The ghost was still standing in the same spot. She marveled at how beautiful the atoms were that made up his form, both transparent and shimmering at the same time. Lin smiled, amused by the fact that tourists and island natives bustled by the ghost with no idea that a spirit stood so close to them and for a moment, she felt lucky to be able to see the ones who had passed. She gave Sebastian a slight nod.

"What's he doing?" Viv's voice sounded less shaky.

"Just looking over here."

"Is he communicating with you?"

"No, just looking." Lin kept her eyes locked on Sebastian's. "Let's stand quietly in case he tries to tell me something." Her hand went to her necklace and she ran her finger over the horseshoe on the pendant. The necklace was once owned by Sebastian's wife, Emily.

As Lin watched, it seemed that the particles that made up the ghost's body started to glow brighter and she couldn't tell if it was just the daylight and the way the sun was striking the atoms that made him glow or if it was the atoms themselves that sparkled so brightly. She felt like she couldn't take her eyes off of the ghost even though the gleam was becoming so glaring that it almost caused pain to look at him.

Unconsciously, Lin raised her hand to shield her eyes and then the ghost's light started to dim. The atoms began their now familiar swirling and Lin knew Sebastian was about to disappear. The first time the ghost had shown up in her yard several months ago, he had frightened and alarmed Lin and she hoped that he would never appear again, but now, when he made one of his rare appearances, her heart filled with happiness and when he left, a twinge of sadness pinched her.

"He's gone." Lin blinked several times at the spot where the ghost had stood.

"Did he tell you anything? Why did he come?" Viv let go of her cousin's arm.

Lin shrugged. "I'm not sure why he came. He didn't tell me anything."

"These ghosts," Viv huffed. She led the way up the sidewalk to the center of Nantucket town. "Why can't they be more straightforward? Everything's a guessing game. Everything is a puzzle. What if we're not good at puzzles? Well, you're good at puzzles, but you know what I mean."

While her cousin continued with her fussing, Lin couldn't help but smile. It didn't matter that Viv was right about the spirits, the ghosts did things in their own way and in their own time.

The only thing Lin could do was try to figure out what it all meant.

\*\*\*

Walking up the street to Viv's bookstore, Lin spotted Anton hurrying down the sidewalk towards them. The historian had his head down and looked deep in thought as he stepped briskly around the people strolling along. Anton carried a black leather folder under his arm and was about to enter the bookstore, when Lin called to him. He stopped abruptly and glanced around suspiciously not realizing who spoke his name.

Lin and Viv approached.

"It's just us," Viv told the short, wiry man. On her way inside to check on her employees, she said, "Lin saw Sebastian Coffin."

Anton looked wide-eyed at Lin. "Where did you see him?"

"Are you going in?" Lin gestured to the bookstore entryway. "Are you meeting Libby?"

Anton shook his head. "I'm not meeting anyone. Libby's gone to the mainland. I was going to get a coffee and do some paperwork at one of the tables. I have a meeting later on in town."

"Can you spare a few minutes to talk?"

"Absolutely." Anton stepped back for Lin to enter. They found a table in the corner, got cups of tea at the counter, and settled in their chairs.

"Tell me what happened with Sebastian, Carolin." Anton's eyes were like lasers.

Lin explained her and Viv's visit to Lacey Frye's basket shop. "When we stepped outside, Sebastian was across the street watching us."

"Did he communicate?"

"No. I didn't get any sensations about why he might have appeared. He stood for only a few seconds watching me and then he was gone." Lin gave a shrug. Whenever she saw a spirit, she always wished she had more information to share with Viv and Libby and Anton. Her experiences with the ghosts often felt inadequate and unhelpful to whatever needed to be solved.

"Hmmm." Anton stroked his chin. "Why today? Why right then and there?"

"I have no idea." Lin hoped to get some information about Lacey. "Do you know Lacey Frye?"

"Yes, I know her. I haven't seen her for some time. She's had health problems all of her life. The poor woman looks much older than her years. I think she's in her mid to late fifties, but her illnesses have aged her at least ten years. I'm impressed that she's still working."

"Do you know anything about her? She asked me a lot of questions about what I saw and heard the evening of the robbery."

Anton shifted in his seat. "I don't know much about her. I know her side of the family has some Wampanoag blood, but she only has one distant ancestor related to the tribe. She's skilled at making the baskets, in fact, she's better than Nathan Long ... she's had that shop in town for years ... twenty years probably."

"She doesn't seem to like Martha Hillman." Lin shared her observation with Anton.

Anton let out a sigh and leaned back against the chair. "There are many people who don't care for Martha."

"Do they have reason not to like her?" Lin watched Anton's face.

Anton flapped at the air with his hand. "I can't speak for others. Martha can be abrasive, forceful, demanding. She can rub people the wrong way. Martha has definite opinions which sometimes don't jive with what others think or want." Anton looked thoughtful. "Some people think *I* can be abrasive." His eyes twinkled. "That might come as a surprise to you."

The corner of Lin's mouth turned up.

"I don't think it's a bad thing to have strong ideas and opinions." Anton went on. "I think it's important to bring people together who think differently, get different perspectives and outlooks."

Lin gave a nod. "Have you heard about some missing money at a non-profit that was never found? It happened years ago. Martha worked there."

Anton's right eyebrow went up. "I know about it. Marguerite Reed was let go from her position because of the incident."

"Leonard's wife." Lin nodded. "She was cleared of wrongdoing though."

"Yes." Anton gazed across the café. "Leonard feels that the dismissal without cause led to his wife's death. She was killed in an accident on the mainland when returning from a job interview."

Lin saw the historian's Adam's apple rise and fall as he swallowed hard.

"The hand of fate." Anton's eyes looked moist. "Marguerite was a lovely woman. She did some volunteer work with a group of us when we were trying to start the cultural museum."

Something pinged in Lin's chest. "What kind of work?"

"She helped with the bookkeeping, did some financial projections. We were trying to raise money to start the new museum. There was a building that we were considering buying, but the numbers didn't work, so we had to abandon the idea." Anton rubbed his forehead. "We had to put the idea of the museum on hold for a few years."

"So you were part of the original group that worked on founding the museum?" Lin sat up. "Who else was in the group?"

"Marguerite, Martha Hillman." Anton paused. "It was so long ago and I've been on so many committees, let me think. Oh, Lacey Frye was involved as well … and Nathan Long. A few others you wouldn't know."

"All these people's names come up when I ask about the robbery of the basket," Lin observed.

Anton's eyes widened in surprise. "Well, these are all people who have been involved in the community for years, they've served on committees, volunteered, fundraised."

Lin leaned forward. "Do any of those people have motive to steal the basket?"

Anton's jaw dropped. "I … I," he stammered. "I

would never consider that these people would do such a thing. They care so much for the island, the town." The historian seemed to be struggling with the idea that someone he'd worked closely with had done wrong. Little beads of perspiration formed on his forehead. "Oh, my. I suppose it's possible, however disturbing the idea may be."

"What about Martha Hillman? She worked at the non-profit when the money went missing. She works at the cultural museum and was the one who discovered the basket missing." Lin made quotation marks in the air with her fingers when she repeated, "'Discovered.' Maybe Martha didn't *discover* it was gone. Maybe Martha stole it."

"Oh." Anton blinked. "Oh." He shook his head. "No, it couldn't be Martha. She wouldn't steal the basket. She works so hard."

Lin made a face. "People who work hard are capable of wrongdoing."

Anton pressed the small white paper napkin against his brow. "Next, you'll be suspecting me."

Lin hated to see the man in such distress and wanted to lighten the mood so she raised one eyebrow in mock concern and leaned closer. "Did *you* steal it?"

Anton nearly toppled from his chair. He gripped the table staring at Lin for a moment, missing the fact that she was kidding when suddenly it dawned on him that she was joking. "Carolin," he chided her. "You almost gave me a heart attack."

Lin grinned. "You reacted so strongly to my question about stealing the basket that I wondered if maybe I *should* put you on the list of suspects."

Anton pushed his glasses up his nose, studied Lin's face, and then relaxed. "I didn't realize you had such a wicked sense of humor, Carolin."

Lin couldn't resist teasing the man one more time. She gave Anton a sly look. "Who says I'm joking?"

## CHAPTER 12

Lin carried a platter of salad to the deck table just as Viv came into the house through the front door with a big bowl of her homemade meatballs and spaghetti sauce. She and Lin went into the kitchen to heat them on the stovetop and Queenie found Nicky on the deck and the two ran into the back field to do some exploring.

"I think Queenie is really a dog." Lin took out a wooden spoon and stirred the sauce and meatballs in the pot.

"Or, Nicky is really a cat." Viv put a mousse pie in the fridge.

The two chuckled. The dog and cat had been fast friends since Lin and her little rescue dog returned to the island several months ago to make Nantucket their home.

Viv poured a glass of wine and sat at the kitchen island. "What did Anton have to say about you seeing Sebastian?"

Lin blew out a sigh. "Really? Not much. There isn't much to say when a ghost shows up and just stares at me. I didn't pick up on any message or clue or whatever he might have been trying to send me." Lin's shoulders drooped. "I don't know why I have this skill. I feel like I'm deaf to receiving messages from the ghosts." She turned the burner's heat down to simmer, covered the pot, and joined Viv at the counter.

"Remember right before Liliana died and I went to meet her?" Liliana had been a friend of Libby and Anton and she and Lin shared the gift of being able to see spirits. "Liliana told me that I'd get better at communicating with the ghosts, but how? She said I would take her place. How can I ever do that? I feel like a big dummy."

A gentle smile spread over Viv's lips. "You are not a dummy. Things take time. Liliana didn't expect you to fill her shoes right away. When I first picked up a guitar or sat at the piano, I couldn't play a song. I just plunked out notes. No one is good at anything without practice." She chuckled. "Without a *whole lot* of practice. It must be the same with your talent. The more ghosts you see, the better you'll get at picking up what they have to tell you."

Lin leaned on the island. "How are you so smart?"

"I was born that way." Viv sipped from her wine glass.

"You didn't need to practice to get so smart?" Lin eyed her cousin. "Doesn't that negate your statement that every talent must be honed and practiced?"

Viv threw her head back and laughed. "Now who's acting like a smarty pants?"

Before Lin jumped down from her perch on the stool, she gave her cousin a little poke in the side. "Me."

The girls sat on the deck with dinner plates of spaghetti and meatballs, garlic bread, and salad. They chattered about their boyfriends, a movie they'd recently seen, and plans to go to the beach together late Saturday afternoon. When the sun slipped below the horizon and darkness fell over the yard, Lin lit the candles on the table and brought out the chocolate mousse pie.

Lin filled her glass with sparkling water and passed the bottle to Viv. "Anton told me that years ago, a group of people we've been talking about or who we've recently met, worked together to start the cultural museum. The finances wouldn't work and they had to shelve the idea for a few years."

"Who was involved?" Viv lifted a forkful of the pie to her mouth.

"Anton. Martha Hillman. Lacey Frye. Nathan Long. Leonard's wife, Marguerite."

Viv lowered her fork. "All of those people?"

"Anton said others were involved, but that I probably wouldn't know who they were."

"So those people go way back. They've known each other a long time." Viv's eyebrows knitted together in thought. "And now, Marguerite is dead, Martha and Nathan are involved with the museum, and Lacey doesn't seem to care for either Martha or Nathan. What about Anton? Does he have anything bad to say about any of them?"

"No, he really doesn't. When I proposed that one of them could be involved in the theft, he was horrified to think that it was possible."

"I wonder what the relationship is between those people." Viv tapped the side of her face.

"And I wonder what the relationship *used to be* between them." Lin made eye contact with her cousin. "Does someone bear a grudge towards one of the group? Could someone have stolen the basket to make one of them look bad? Tarnish their reputation?"

Viv's eyes went wide and she leaned forward on the table. "Or, what if they're all working together? What if they planned the whole thing together?"

"For what purpose?" Lin looked confused.

"Sell the basket and split the money? Set up someone they hate to take the fall? It hasn't been that long since the crime occurred. Maybe the thief will try to pin the robbery on one of the group?"

"What a tangled web." Lin put her chin in her hand. "We need to find out what the relationships are between them. Anton is innocent. He's only involved because he helped secure the loan of the basket from his curator friend." Lin sat up. "Oh. What if one of them tries to set up Anton? What if one of them is out to get Anton for some reason? They must have known that Anton was friends with the curator on the mainland and could use his influence to bring the basket to the cultural museum on loan. What if one of them has a grudge against Anton? What if this whole thing was done to ruin Anton's reputation?"

"That's terrible." Viv scowled. "We need to suggest this to Anton so he can be on guard."

Lin nodded. "We also need to talk to Martha and Lacey and Nathan. Ask some questions about the past, and the present. See if we can figure out if there's bad blood between any of them."

Nicky and Queenie had been resting on the grass beyond the deck when they suddenly stood up and stared at the side yard.

"What's wrong with them?" Viv glanced at the animals.

Just as Lin was going to get up to see what the cat and dog were looking at, Anton Wilson dashed around from the other side of the house and hurried to the deck. "I thought you'd be back here. I need to talk to you." Anton plopped onto one of the deck chairs. His skin looked ashen.

"What's wrong with you?" Lin could feel the nervous energy flowing out of the man.

"The police came to see me. They asked me a million questions. I thought I might pass out."

Lin poured Anton a glass of sparkling water and handed it to him. "They were doing some follow-up questions?"

Anton shook his head. "Well, maybe, but their tone was different this time. When they first questioned me at the museum on the night the basket went missing, they were polite. Today they were downright rude, accusatory, condescending."

"What did they ask?" Viv looked at Anton's pale face.

"I think they believe that I'm the thief." Anton sucked in a breath and sat straighter. "They think that I secured the loan of the basket from the mainland museum in order to steal it."

"Oh for heaven's sake." Viv groaned.

"Did the police actually say that or are you letting your mind run wild?" Lin eyed the troubled historian.

"They didn't come right out and say it. It was their manner, their tone, subtle things."

"They can't pin this on you, Anton." Lin was careful to keep her voice calm. "You were with me. I can be your alibi."

Anton looked down his nose at Lin. "You were with me when we went inside the museum. You were not with me prior to entering. We met on the steps. You can't be my alibi unless you lie."

"Lin won't lie." Viv's voice was forceful.

Anton's face screwed up. "I would never ask Carolin to do such a thing."

"Where were you before I met you in front of the museum?" Lin asked.

## A Haunted Theft

"I was at home and then I walked to the museum." He shook his head. "I was alone until I met you so I have no one who can vouch for me being at home."

"Did the police actually accuse you?" Viv turned to face Anton.

"Not in so many words." Anton took a long swallow from his glass.

"So they aren't charging you. Good." Lin made eye contact with the historian. "It might be a good idea to talk to a lawyer."

Anton stopped breathing for a few seconds, and then he blinked and nodded. "Yes. I'll do that."

"It will make you feel better to have advice and representation." Viv gave the man a smile. "You haven't done anything wrong, but I understand how upsetting it might be to be falsely accused." Several months ago, shortly after Lin returned to the island, Viv was questioned by police about the murder of a Nantucket man and she worried that she would be arrested for his death.

Viv's phone buzzed with an incoming text. She read it and looked up, surprised. "It's from John. He's just leaving the office. He's on his way over. He says he has some news to tell us."

"News?" Lin's face lit up. "Maybe there's been an arrest. Maybe the case is solved." She smiled at Anton. "Then your worries would be over."

"John can't get here fast enough." Anton stood up and started to pace around the deck.

Lin and Viv chatted nervously to pass the time until John arrived. They tried to draw Anton into the conversation, but he only replied to their comments and questions with a few words.

After ten minutes had passed, Nicky and Queenie darted across the deck to the door leading to the living room and stared through the screen into the house.

Viv turned to look. "It must be John."

"The front door's unlocked," Lin said.

John rushed through the house and out to the deck.

Anton said nothing, just stood waiting for John to tell the news.

"Is the case solved?" Viv walked towards her boyfriend and took his hand. "Do they know who stole the basket?"

"What?" John looked confused for a moment. "No, it's not solved at all."

Lin's heart sank.

"What do you have to tell us then?" Anton asked. His face was pale.

"Someone from the museum was found dead."

Lin leaped to her feet as she, Viv, and Anton all spoke at once.

"What?!"

"Dead?"

"Who?"

"It's that woman who worked there. She's dead." John looked around at the three faces staring at him. "It's Martha Hillman."

## CHAPTER 13

Lin, Viv, John, and Anton sat down at the deck table. John removed his tie, shoved it into the pocket of his suit jacket before slipping it off and hanging it over the back of his chair. Picking up Viv's empty wine glass, he poured some from the bottle, and took a swallow.

"Who told you?" Viv questioned. "Your friend at the police station?"

John nodded. "Ms. Hillman was found at home. I don't know how long she'd been dead."

"I saw her this morning going into the museum so it had to have happened sometime today." Anton's hand was shaking as he sipped water from his glass.

"Was it a heart attack?" Lin folded her arms on the tabletop and leaned forward.

John took a breath before answering. "No." He shook his head. "She was found in her garage." He looked at each person around the table. "The car was running."

Anton sucked in a quick breath and moaned.

"Suicide?"

"Oh, dear." Viv's hand flew to her cheek. "Oh, no."

"Suicide?" Lin's mind was racing. "That makes it seem that she was running away from something ... or that she couldn't face something."

Viv's eyes widened. "The basket. Either Martha stole it or she knows something that she couldn't deal with."

Anton looked like he'd shrunk in his seat. His shoulders drooped and his head tilted forward as he looked down at the deck flooring in a spaced out state.

Lin put her hand on the man's arm. "I'm sorry. You'd known her for many years."

Anton's lower lip trembled. "We weren't friends, really, only acquaintances, but friendly to each other." His hand passed over his face. "What in the world would cause Martha to do such a thing?"

Lin could think of a couple of things, but decided not to voice them.

"Who found her?" Viv asked John.

"The man who did her lawn. He arrived to cut the grass. He was running late, but since it was still light out, he decided to catch up on some of his work. The man heard the sound of a car engine running in the garage. The door was down and closed. He looked in through the garage window and called the police."

"Ugh." Viv shook her head slowly. "What an

awful thing to find."

Something about the whole thing picked at Lin. "It certainly makes Martha look guilty or at least, involved in some way in the theft of the basket, doesn't it?"

Anton gave a little nod and said sadly, "It does indeed."

"Hmmm." Lin tapped the tabletop absent-mindedly with her index finger.

"What?" Viv turned towards Lin and then her eyes narrowed realizing what her cousin might be implying. "Oh."

Lin's jaw muscle gave a slight twitch. "What if it's *supposed* to look like a suicide?"

A puzzled expression creased Anton's forehead and then his confusion lifted. "Oh, my."

John looked at Lin. "Huh. Interesting. A definite possibility."

Lin voiced what now everyone was pondering. "Someone may have killed Martha. Someone involved in the robbery could have staged the whole thing to look like a suicide. Maybe Martha knew who stole the basket. She could even have been involved in the theft in some way and her partner wanted to get rid of her. Maybe she was about to go to the police. Who knows? But her death may not have been suicide at all."

"Wow," Viv said softly. "What in the world is going on?"

"More questions and no answers." Lin let out a

sigh. The case was becoming more complicated by the day. "If the medical examiner rules it a suicide then Martha will be considered the thief. But where's the basket?"

"Martha could have sold it already," John surmised.

Viv offered a possibility. "It could be hidden somewhere."

Feeling a chill, Lin rubbed her arms and glanced around to see if any ghosts were making an appearance, but no shimmering spirits could be seen. "If Martha was murdered over the antique basket, it makes the robbery much more serious since someone is willing to kill for it."

"The whole thing is giving me a headache." Viv got up to go inside to the kitchen to get another bottle of seltzer and a glass.

When Viv returned to her seat, Lin spoke. "We were talking earlier." She looked directly at Anton. "A number of names have come up in connection to the cultural museum ... it's founding, the exhibition, and the robbery. We wondered if someone might bear a grudge against one of the people involved with those things. Could someone from the founding committee be angry over an issue from the past? Has someone held a deep-seated resentment that has built up over all these years? Could a member of the group be a target for some reason?"

Anton winced at the thought. He looked weak

and frail. Lin's words seemed to fall over him like a heavy weight. One of his skinny shoulders shrugged. "I need to think. I'm good for nothing at the moment. I need to go home and rest. Then I'll be able to put my mind to it." Anton pushed himself from his seat.

Nicky whined at the man.

John stood. "I'll drive you home."

Anton was about to protest, but was too low in energy to argue so he and John left the girls standing on the deck. Lin and Viv wished the historian well and thanked John for ushering Anton to his home. They cleared off the table and went inside to make tea.

Sitting at the kitchen island, Viv sighed. "What a mess. The whole thing is so complicated."

Lin set the tea kettle on the burner. "I was feeling pretty sure that Martha Hillman was responsible for the theft. I suppose it's still possible that she stole the basket, especially if she committed suicide." Removing two mugs from the cabinet, she turned towards her cousin. "I don't know why and I don't have anything to base my idea on, but I think Martha was murdered." Lin's eyelids looked heavy.

Viv stared at Lin for a few seconds. "I would never doubt your feelings."

"I didn't like the woman." Lin took milk out of the fridge. "She seemed cocky and superior. Anton said she could be abrasive. But none of that is reason to kill her."

"The reason she's dead must have more to it than Martha having a snotty personality." Viv had a weariness in her voice. "She either did something or knew something."

The corners of Lin's mouth turned up. "That narrows it down."

Realizing that what she'd said covered every possibility, Viv smiled. "How are we going to figure this out?"

Lin's blue eyes widened. "Remember when we were in the hall outside Martha's office and we heard her say things about someone she fired?"

Viv perked up. "Right. If we can find out who got fired, then we can talk to her, find out what she knows." She frowned. "The person who got fired could be the one who killed Martha." Viv looked over her shoulder into the dark living room.

Lin couldn't help a chuckle escaping from her throat. "I don't think the person who killed Martha is lurking in my living room."

Viv batted her hand in the air. "You know how I am." She checked over her shoulder one more time. Lowering her voice, she asked, "Did you see any ghosts when we were all outside talking about Martha?"

"No, nothing." Lin shook her head.

Viv harrumphed. "Why can't they be more helpful? The ghosts should show up and nod when we're on the right track."

Lin poured the tea and carried the mugs to the kitchen island. "I don't think we can hope for help like that." Climbing onto the stool next to Viv, Lin let out a sigh. "I haven't seen the Wampanoag ghost since I was in the garden of the cultural museum talking to Nathan Long about the landscaping job."

"He'll show up again." Viv added milk and sugar to her tea. "They always do." She sipped the hot beverage. "Have you heard from Nathan about whether or not you've got the job?"

"He's supposed to let me know tomorrow. The board supposedly voted this morning."

Viv lifted her mug. "Martha must have been there for the vote. Anton said he saw her going into the museum this morning."

"I'm sure she voted against," Lin said. "She thought spending money on the garden was wasteful."

"Do you think that her negative vote might have been the last straw? Maybe someone on the board had enough of Martha obstructing their ideas." Viv eyed her cousin. "Maybe Martha's death has absolutely nothing to do with the stolen basket."

"I didn't think of that." Lin blinked. "Could a person be that angry with a board member that they would commit murder?"

"Crazy things happen. I don't think it can be ruled out."

The girls sipped their tea in silence for a while.

## A Haunted Theft

"I'm feeling antsy." Lin slipped off the stool. "I feel like I need to be doing something."

Viv didn't respond, but shifted her eyes suspiciously to her cousin afraid of what she was going to say next.

"Want to go for a drive?" Lin asked.

"Where to?" Viv's voice sounded hesitant.

"Want to ride by Martha Hillman's house?"

Viv groaned. "Why? You won't be able to get near it. The police will be all over the place."

"I know. I just thought if I drove by, maybe I'd pick up on something … or see something."

"I suppose that would be okay." Viv drank the last of her tea.

Nicky had been listening and let out a woof of agreement.

"Just don't go dragging me through the woods to get to the back of Martha's house." Viv looked at the dog. "If that's what your owner wants to do, then it's your job to go along. The cat and I will stay in the truck."

Nicky woofed again.

Lin used her phone to search for Martha's address. "Got it. She lives just outside of town off the road to Madaket."

"Great," Viv deadpanned. "The last time you went to a house off of that road you found a dead body." Viv was referring to a previous case that they'd stuck their noses into about a month ago. Rinsing her mug in the sink, she added, "You might want to stay off that road from now on."

"I'll keep that in mind." Lin chuckled as she led her cousin, the dog, and the cat out of the house and into her truck.

# CHAPTER 14

"We could have walked over." Viv watched the scenery go by as Lin drove her truck to the neighborhood just outside of Nantucket town.

"I thought of that, but we have the cat and I didn't want a dog to bother her and besides, we can sit in the car and watch what's going on."

When they were getting close to Martha Hillman's Cape-style house, Lin and Viv could see the blue lights of a police car flashing up ahead. Lin pulled the truck to the curb behind a line of other vehicles a few houses down from Martha's. Small groups of people had formed here and there on the sidewalks to watch the proceedings and gossip.

"News travels fast," Viv observed.

"We can't get any closer with the truck. I think we'll have to get out and walk up the street."

"Nicky and Queenie will be fine." Viv looked at the dog and cat. "Guard the truck, you two. We won't be long."

Lin and Viv approached the first cluster of gawkers. They didn't recognize anyone they knew.

Viv asked for news even though she knew the basics of what had happened. People supplied some information.

"A woman committed suicide."

"Her lawn guy found her in the garage."

"She worked at the cultural museum."

"Some people think she was the one who stole that valuable basket."

Viv asked, "When was she found?"

"A few hours ago."

"Have they taken her away?" Lin wondered if Martha had been left in the car where she'd died as the police investigated the scene.

"An ambulance drove away about an hour ago."

Viv nodded at the people and she and her cousin moved down the street to get closer to the house.

"There aren't many streetlamps. It's hard to make out who's hanging around out here in the dark." Lin linked arms with Viv.

As they walked, they looked from side to side trying to see who was there. When they were almost across from the house, Viv stopped short. She nodded to a spot across the street. "Isn't that Nathan Long?"

Lin squinted. "It looks like him."

Nathan was swaying slightly from foot to foot while speaking intently with a tall, lean woman. Occasionally, they would glance up the driveway to Martha's house. The tall woman had a white tissue in one hand and she dabbed at her eyes every few seconds. A police officer walked down the drive towards Nathan and the woman, said a few words, and then led them up to the house.

"Huh," Lin said. "Why are they being taken inside?"

"Maybe Nathan saw Martha earlier in the day. Maybe the police want to ask for some details."

Lin noticed a woman with a long black ponytail straddling a bicycle. "Isn't that Mary Frye?" Lin and Viv walked over and said hello.

"How sad," Mary commented. "I can't believe it. It's a terrible shock."

"How did you hear?" Viv asked.

"I stopped in town to buy a water bottle. People in the store were talking about it. At first, I thought they must be wrong."

"It's an awful shock when someone you know dies," Lin said.

"It's not just that." Mary switched off the blinking light on her handle bars. "Ms. Hillman is the last person I would ever think would take her own life."

Lin tilted her head. "What was it about Martha that made you think that way?"

Mary looked at Lin. "She was ... forceful, confidant."

"She may have been depressed for a long time and hid it well from everyone," Viv said softly. "I guess we don't always know someone or what they might be feeling."

Mary seemed to be processing what Viv said. "It doesn't fit though." Mary gave a shrug. "It just doesn't fit."

Lin took a step closer to Mary. "Who was the person who got fired recently from the museum? I know Martha let someone go not long ago."

Something flickered over Mary's face. "I didn't know that someone got fired."

Lin wanted to sigh, but took a different tack. "Maybe I'm wrong then. Didn't someone give notice? Someone resigned?"

"Oh. Is that who you mean? She didn't get fired. She left for a different position." Mary nodded.

"Who was that?" Lin gave a gentle smile.

"Avery Holden. She'd worked at the museum for quite a while."

"How did you like her? Did she work well with everyone?" Lin kept her innocent smile on her face trying to encourage Mary to be forthcoming.

The same fleeting look that had flickered over Mary's face earlier showed itself for a second and then was gone. "Sure. I liked her a lot." Mary turned her handlebar headlight back on and changed the subject. "Will you be taking the other weaving class I'm giving next week?" She perched on the bike seat.

"I think so." Viv smiled. "I loved the last class we took."

Mary said goodbye and rode away on her bicycle.

## A Haunted Theft

"Do you think Mary knows that Avery Holden got fired?" Viv asked her cousin.

"I sure do," Lin replied. "What do you think?"

"I agree with you. It might be time to look up Avery Holden."

Lin watched the activity still going on up by the house. "Anton must know Avery. I'll ask him."

The girls stood watching for a few more minutes when a woman walking past bumped into Lin and started to apologize profusely until she recognized who she'd run into. "Oh. Lin." Claire Rollins's blonde curls bobbed on her head shining under the light of the streetlamp. The young woman's face muscles were taut and her eyes looked red-rimmed. "I was driving home. I pulled over." She waved her hand and pointed down the street. "Nathan Long called to tell me what happened." Her trembling fingers pushed a stray curl out of her eye. "I can't believe it. Martha killed herself?"

"It could have been an accident." Lin knew it wasn't, but felt the need to offer the possibility.

"An accident?" Claire blinked.

"Maybe Martha drove home. Maybe she wasn't feeling well and passed out in the car before she turned the engine off."

"Oh." Claire looked up the driveway to the garage. Two police officers stood in front of the structure. "Maybe that's what happened. Poor Martha."

Lin remembered that Viv and Claire had never

met and introduced them to one another.

"Was there a board meeting this morning?" Lin asked. "Did you attend?"

Claire turned to Lin and nodded. "Martha was there."

"Did she seem herself?"

Claire thought for several seconds. "She seemed normal. Nothing out of the ordinary. Nothing I noticed anyway."

Viv spoke up. "Did she seem unwell?"

"What?" Claire took a deep breath. "I don't think so." She returned her attention to the officials bustling in and out of the house. Without looking at Lin, Claire said, "You got the contract, by the way, for the landscaping. We voted this morning. Nathan will call you."

"Oh, okay. Thanks." Lin wanted to ask if Martha voted against the project, but she knew the results were probably confidential and anyway, it seemed crass to ask how the dead woman had voted. "Nathan was here a few minutes ago."

"He left?" Claire flicked her eyes to Lin for a second and then turned back to the scene.

Viv spoke up. "The police escorted him into Martha's house."

Claire looked at Viv. "Up to the house? Nathan's inside? Why?"

Viv and Lin both shrugged.

"That's odd, isn't it?" Claire said. "It's a crime scene. Wouldn't bringing people inside contaminate the evidence?"

"They took him to the house," Viv told her, "not into the garage."

"Oh, well, I'd better get going." Claire seemed twitchy and jumpy. She bit her lip and blinked a few times. Lin thought Claire was trying to keep herself from crying. "I'll see you." Claire nodded and headed off down the street.

"She's pretty shook up." Viv watched the young woman walk away.

"Claire is one of my clients now. Martha was at her house the other day."

"She was married to that old guy, what was his name?" Viv asked. "They had like a fifty-year age difference between them, didn't they?"

Lin smiled. "His name was Teddy Rollins. It was probably more like a forty-five- year age difference."

"The guy was ancient. Yuck." Viv shook her head thinking of marrying someone so much older.

"Yuck probably wasn't what Claire said when she inherited old Teddy's billions."

Viv's eyes widened. "Billions?"

"Yup. Now you're seeing things in a new light?" Lin kidded her cousin.

"No pre-nup? No kids or other relatives?"

"Nothing. Just oodles of money. The word on the street is that everything went to Claire."

"Well, well. Claire is very clever, isn't she?" Viv watched a newly arrived police car speed up

Martha's driveway. "Why have I never thought to find a rich boyfriend?"

Lin chuckled. "Didn't you think John was wealthy when you met him?"

"No." Viv shook her head. "I fell for cute, smart, and kind." She gave Lin a mock sad face. "I wasn't thinking."

The girls wandered around the gawkers for another ten minutes. "You want to stay longer?" Viv asked.

"I guess not. I'm not picking up on anything."

Viv lowered her voice. "No ghosts?"

"Nothing. Let's go back to the truck." The two headed down the dark street in the direction they'd come. Lin said, "Claire really seemed jumpy and shook up, didn't she?"

"Isn't that normal after what just happened?" Viv questioned.

Lin gave her cousin a look.

"Oh." Viv sighed. "Maybe Claire needs to go on the suspect list."

## CHAPTER 15

Before heading to her first client of the day, Lin stopped at Anton's house to see how he was holding up and to ask him about Avery Holden. When Anton opened the door, his face looked weary and drawn. Nicky rubbed against the man's leg causing Anton to bend and pat the top of the dog's head and Lin could see some of the tension in the historian's body melt away. "A fine creature." Anton praised the little brown dog.

They headed for the kitchen and sat at the long wooden table.

"How are you doing?" Lin's eyes were full of concern.

"Yesterday was a nightmare." Anton rubbed his temple and adjusted his black-rimmed glasses. "I barely slept. I kept thinking of Martha. I kept replaying my meeting with the police."

"You know the police have to cover every angle." Lin's voice was gentle. "Talking to you again doesn't mean they suspect you. When they talk to people, they can find out small things that can lead to the criminal."

"That's hard to remember when you are the one being questioned."

Lin nodded. "Like we said last night, if it makes you feel better, talk to an attorney and get some advice."

"I think I will." Anton sat up. "Oh, my manners. What can I get you? Tea? A cold drink?"

Lin smiled. Even when consumed with worry and upset, Anton was the perfect host. "A cold drink would be nice."

Anton placed a bowl of cool water on the floor for the dog and bustled about cutting a lime into slices, taking out ice cubes, and pouring homemade iced tea into the tall glasses that had sailing ships etched onto the sides. The ice cubes clinked as Anton carried the refreshing beverages to the table. He arranged cookies on a plate and put them in the center of the table. Before sitting down again, he hurried to one of the kitchen cabinets and took out a small bag of dog treats. Nicky cocked his head when he heard the rustle of the bag. Anton put two biscuits on a white plate and set it before the dog.

"If you treat him like a king," Lin said, "then Nicky will abandon me and move in here with you."

"I wouldn't mind that one bit." Anton watched the dog enjoy the treats.

"Have you talked to Libby?"

"She's on the mainland for a few more days."

Hearing that Libby was still away caused a

momentary pulse of panic to surge through Lin's body and she gave herself a slight shake to throw it off. She knew they could just call Libby if they needed her and Lin suggested to Anton that he ring her to tell her what's been going on.

"I should wait until she comes back. I don't want to bother her."

"I think you should tell her about Martha, at least." Lin thought Libby should be notified about the death of the island resident although she'd probably heard it on the news already. The real reason Lin wanted Anton to talk to her was so that Libby could hear the worry in his voice and offer him some comfort and advice.

"You're right. I'll call her."

"Can I ask you some questions about people?" Lin watched Anton's face. She didn't want a discussion to cause him more upset.

"Are the questions related to what's been happening?"

Lin nodded.

"Ask. Maybe talking about things will make me feel less helpless."

"I don't think Martha killed herself. I just have this strong feeling that someone made the whole thing look like a suicide. Maybe I'm completely wrong, but I feel it, Anton. When I think about Martha killing herself, I get a weird sensation like you might feel when you're lost. But when I think that someone did this to her, I get a surge of energy that flows through my muscles. It makes me feel like I'm on the right track."

Anton stared at Lin.

"I'm not describing it correctly." Lin started to explain it in a different way when Anton cut her off.

"I understand." Anton's looked less tense. "The spirits must be sending you these impulses. I know something similar about a woman who could see ghosts like you do. She got sensations, almost like silent messages. She knew the feelings were sent to her by the spirits."

Lin asked carefully, "Are you talking about Liliana?"

A slight smile showed on Anton's lips. "Yes."

A ping of joy danced in Lin's heart. Maybe her ability to see ghosts was expanding to receiving small messages or feelings from the spirits that would help direct her and nudge her onto the right path when trying to find clues. A smile spread over her face. "I need to be more open to such sensations and not dismiss them."

Anton nodded. His face looked hopeful. "What questions do you want to ask me?"

"Do you know Avery Holden?"

"Of course. She worked at the cultural museum."

"She got fired?" Lin wondered if anyone besides Martha and Avery knew that Avery had been let go from her position.

"No. She left of her own accord."

Lin asked, "Did a different employee get fired recently?"

Anton's lips pursed for a moment. "No one has left their position at the museum besides Avery."

Lin told the historian what she and Viv heard when standing outside Martha Hillman's closed office door.

Anton pushed back against his chair. "What could she have meant? What was Martha talking about? Who was she talking to?"

"Those are all things I've asked myself." Lin's forehead creased. "Can you tell me about Avery?"

"Avery is hardworking, takes her job seriously. She always put in lots of extra hours. She has a master's degree in art history from Yale."

"What was her position at the museum?"

"She started as an assistant curator and ended up sort of a jack-of-all-trades. Avery had a hand in every aspect of the functioning of the museum."

"How old is she?" Lin was making mental notes about the woman.

"Mid-thirties?"

"Did she get along with Martha?"

Anton frowned. "No. They were often at odds. I always thought it was a shame. Two bright, hardworking people." He shook his head. "They could have been a wonderful team, but...."

"But?"

"Sometimes I got the impression that they deliberately antagonized one another. Oh, it was small things, but nonetheless, it created unnecessary tension and interfered, I thought, with the smooth running of the museum."

"Avery has a new job?"

"No. I was told that she is going to law school."

"Where does she live?"

Anton looked blank. "I don't know."

Lin narrowed her eyes. "I think I should have a talk with Avery. If I can find her."

Anton gave a vigorous nod of his head. "Yes. Then maybe you can find out the source of the animosity between the women and maybe Avery can shed light on what Martha meant about firing an employee."

Lin had lots of questions she hoped to be able to ask Avery Holden, but she wasn't so sure that the former cultural museum employee was going to be forthcoming with any answers. "I don't like saying this, but there are a number of people who might have wanted Martha dead."

"As I said before, she could be very abrasive."

Lin looked pointedly at Anton. "Did any of the people you know hate her enough to want to kill her?"

In a weak voice, Anton said, "Possibly. Probably everyone I can think."

Lin's eyebrows shot up. "I wasn't expecting that answer."

"That doesn't mean anyone would act on their feelings." Anton stood up and started pacing around. Nicky sat up and watched the man go from one end of the room to the other. "People sometimes wish ill on others ... on people who are mean or nasty or don't get along with others, or cause trouble ... oh, for many reasons. It doesn't actually mean they would kill the object of their derision."

"It sounds like Martha has a long history of people not liking her," Lin said. "But what was the impetus now? What happened that pushed someone to kill her now?"

"The stolen basket?"

"That seems to be the key to the mess, doesn't it?" Lin sighed and rested her chin in her hand. "Two questions to answer now. Who stole the basket and who killed Martha Hillman?"

Anton stopped pacing. "One will probably lead to the other."

"Undoubtedly." Lin knew she had a lot of work to do and the path to the answers just kept getting longer and more convoluted.

## CHAPTER 16

Lin and Leonard sat eating their lunch in the shade of a large Maple tree in the backyard of one of their client's homes. Nicky was off sniffing near the marsh that was located at the rear of the property. Lin and her partner were discussing the passing of Martha Hillman.

"You must have been surprised when you heard Martha had died." Lin opened a bottle of orange juice and set it on the grass next to her.

"I'd say more suspicious than surprised." Leonard removed the wrapping from his sandwich.

Lin eyed her partner. "Why suspicious?"

"I knew that woman." Leonard's voice was gruff. "She'd never commit suicide."

"But you hadn't really known her for years. She could have changed. She could have had some difficulties no one was aware of. Maybe she'd had enough."

"Bah." Leonard didn't believe it. "That woman didn't change. And she had difficulties all right. She was a mean-spirited, self-centered, horrible person."

Lin bristled. "Are you just saying this stuff because she was a strong-willed woman?"

Leonard gave Lin a look. "Look, Coffin. My wife was strong-willed. She could do anything. But she wasn't mean. She cared about others. *You* have strong opinions and ideas, but you're not self-centered...." Leonard eyed her. "Well, not most of the time anyway."

Lin's mouth opened in surprise and she bopped him on the arm. "Thanks a lot."

"Martha had a rotten core." Leonard took a swig from his water bottle. "It's awful to say so, but she was an awful person. She thought her needs and wants superseded everyone else's. Her ideas were the best, she was the smartest, she worked the hardest. Marguerite tried to befriend her, but it was impossible. That woman would not kill herself. No way."

"Who did then?"

Leonard shook his head. "The list is probably a mile long. Good luck to the cops trying to solve this one."

Lin let out a sigh. "Yeah."

They ate quietly for a while.

Lin rolled up her empty sandwich bag and put it in her lunch box. "Do you think Martha was the one who stole the antique basket? She was always at the museum. She probably could find opportunity to take it when others were busy or not around."

"Why would she do it though?" Leonard leaned back against the tree's trunk. "That's really the most important question, isn't it?"

"Why wouldn't she do it?" Lin said the words under her breath as she thought it over. "To sell it? For the money?"

"If she got caught, it would ruin her reputation. Would a woman who worked that hard and trampled so many people to get where she wanted risk her hard-won status?"

Lin pushed her hair out of her eyes. "Maybe she hadn't achieved what she wanted. Maybe she felt that her hard work had never been satisfactorily compensated. Maybe she wanted more? Selling the basket would get her a ton of money."

"That's possible." Leonard handed Lin one of the cookies he'd brought in his lunch.

Lin bit into the treat. "Mmmm. Yummy. Where'd you get these?"

"I made them."

"Really?" Lin took another bite and spoke while she chewed. "If you ever tire of landscaping, you can open a bakery."

"I like being outside." Leonard gave Lin a stern look. "You're not supposed to talk with your mouth full."

Lin swallowed. "Sorry. Maybe in the off season you can sell your cookies."

"Maybe not."

Smiling Lin said, "You are a man of many talents and much knowledge." She broke off a piece of the cookie and was about to pop it into her mouth when she asked, "You don't happen to know Avery Holden, do you?"

Lin had looked the woman up on the internet and had come up empty. Avery was listed as an employee of the cultural museum and other entries told of her education and work experience, but there was no phone number or address to be found. Lin planned to ask Anton if he could get the woman's address from someone at the museum.

"Why do you ask?" Leonard had closed his eyes and was still leaning against the tree.

Lin whirled towards her partner. "You know her?"

"Who's asking?"

"Me, for heaven's sake." Lin poked Leonard. "Do you know her or not?"

Leonard's eyelids lifted. "Why are you looking for her, Coffin?"

"I think Martha Hillman fired her from the museum. I want to ask Avery if she knows anything about the basket."

Leonard leveled his gaze at Lin. "Are you looking into the theft?"

"Maybe."

"Martha was probably killed. Maybe she's linked to the robbery. Is it a good idea for you to put yourself in harm's way? This is dangerous stuff."

There was a tinge of anger in the man's voice.

Lin didn't say anything.

"I don't feel like having to find another partner."

"I'll be careful."

Leonard frowned and told her Avery's address.

"How do you know her?" Lin asked.

"Someone gave my number to her. There's a tiny garden off the back of her apartment. She wanted to know what she could plant in the shade."

For a few seconds, Lin pondered the address that Leonard had given her. It sounded familiar, but she couldn't place it.

As if reading her mind, Leonard said, "The apartment is off the back of Lacey Frye's basket shop in town. You know it?"

A shiver ran over Lin's skin. The ghost of Sebastian Coffin had appeared to her right outside of Lacey Frye's shop when Lin and Viv exited the store a few days ago.

*What was he trying to tell her?*

***

Lin and Nicky walked into town and headed to Lacey Frye's shop. After her last client of the day, Lin hurried home, showered, and changed clothes. Her long brown hair was still damp. Approaching the basket shop, Lin's heart started to beat faster. She looked around to see if any ghosts were standing on the sidewalks.

## A Haunted Theft

Lin noticed the brick walkway on the side of the store that led to the back of the building and she and the dog followed it to the rear garden. Leonard said that the spot behind the store was a tiny space and he was right. A large tree grew in the center of the space and hostas were planted around the edges of the small square of lawn. A wrought iron table and two chairs sat under the tree and pots of pink impatiens were placed here and there for bursts of color.

The calm, shady spot relaxed Lin and made the tension start to drain away. She walked to the door of the apartment and knocked. After waiting a few minutes, she raised her hand to knock again when Nicky turned towards the walkway and woofed low and deep in his throat.

A short, slender woman with straight chin-length strawberry-blonde hair came around the corner of the building carrying two grocery bags. She stopped when she spotted Lin at her door.

"Hi." Lin took a step towards the woman. "Avery?"

The woman's face was stern. "Who's asking?"

"I'm Lin Coffin. I was wondering if I could speak to you. I'd just take a few minutes of your time."

The woman advanced, but looked like she didn't trust Lin. "I have plenty of time. I'm not sure I have anything to say though."

Nicky whined at the woman.

Lin didn't know how to respond to Avery's

statement. Finally she asked, "Would you be willing to listen for a few minutes?"

Avery stared at Lin and then said, "I don't let strangers into my house." She nodded to the two wrought-iron chairs. "You want to sit out here?"

When they were settled, Lin told the woman that she was Leonard's landscaping partner and that he had met with Avery not long ago about how to plant the rear yard.

"He was helpful." Avery gestured around the space. "This is the result of his advice. The woman who gave me the apartment has been kind to me. I wanted to do this for her."

"It's lovely."

"What do you want to talk to me about?" Avery held Lin's eyes with her own.

Lin decided not to beat around the bush. "I'd like to talk to you about your job at the cultural museum."

One of the woman's eyebrows went up. "My former job."

"I heard that you're going to law school."

"I always wanted to study law. I think it'll be a good addition to my experience."

Lin looked Avery in the eyes. "Did Martha Hillman fire you?"

It felt like a full minute went by and Lin was sure that Avery wasn't going to answer, but then she spoke. "Yes."

"Why?"

"Why do you want to know?" Avery tilted her head slightly to the side.

Lin took in a deep breath and told the woman what she and Viv had heard in the hallway of the cultural museum while standing outside Martha Hillman's closed office door. "Then Martha said 'do something and get it off the island before someone finds out.'"

"I don't know what she meant by that. I'm not going to tell you why she fired me." Avery shifted in her seat and Lin thought she was about to get up.

Lin blurted out the next question. "Did you steal the antique basket?"

Avery grunted. "No, I did not."

Lin shot questions out rapid-fire. "Do you know who *did* steal it?"

"No."

"Was Martha trying to pin the theft on you?"

"I don't know." Avery looked flustered. "No."

"I've heard that you and Martha didn't get along."

A shadow of annoyance flicked over Avery's face. "No, we did not."

Lin tried again. "Why did Martha fire you?"

Avery's voice was firm. "I'm not going to tell you."

"Do you think Martha killed herself?"

A grunt escaped from Avery's throat. "How would I know?"

Lin said. "I think someone killed her and staged

it to look like she committed suicide.'

"Maybe you're right." Avery leaned down to pick up her grocery bags. "Now I need to get these things put away." She stood.

"Can I talk to you again another time?" Lin got out of her chair.

"Maybe." Avery headed to her front door and pulled her key from her pocket. "Maybe not."

Lin moved slowly to the walkway that led to the front of the building with Nicky at her heels. "Thanks for talking with me." She heard the squeak of the hinges when Avery pushed her apartment door open.

Just as Lin was rounding the corner, Avery called to her, "You know, some people aren't what they seem. You better watch your back."

A chill raced down Lin's spine.

## CHAPTER 17

Hurrying to the sidewalk, Lin saw movement at the front of the basket shop and turned to see Lacey Frye unlocking the door. Lacey looked surprised when she saw Lin coming from the rear of her property.

Lacey nodded a greeting. "Were you visiting Avery?"

"Just for a few minutes." A strange pulse of adrenaline washed over Lin and she didn't understand why.

Lacey's silver-gray braid hung over her shoulder. "You're friends?"

"No. We just met. I needed to ask her something."

The wrinkled skin on Lacey's face drooped a bit at the jowls and her shoulders were stooped as she stood by the door, but there was an intelligence and energy that emanated from the woman. "Did you find out what you wanted to know?"

Even though Lacey's questions made her feel uneasy, Lin shook her head and replied, "Not really."

Lacey eyed Lin. "That was too bad about Martha Hillman."

"Yes. It was a shock." Lin took a few steps towards the street.

"I hope they figure out what's going on soon. The theft ... a death." Lacey let out a sigh and gave Lin a quick nod before entering her store.

***

Lin scurried away and headed up Main Street with her head practically spinning from Lacey's questions and her brief visit with Avery Holden. She nearly stumbled into Viv's house and when Viv turned around and saw her cousin's pale face and worried expression, she rushed to her side.

"I met Avery Holden," Lin managed. "I don't know why I feel so shook up."

"What did she say to you?" Viv maneuvered Lin to the deck and sat her at the table. She brought her cousin a glass of sparkling water.

"Not much really." Lin rubbed her forehead. "When I think about it, she basically avoided almost all of my questions. She admitted that Martha fired her, but she wouldn't say what the circumstances were that brought about the firing." Lin shook her head. "That's understandable. It's personal. She doesn't know me. Why confide anything in a stranger?" She looked across the yard, thinking. "I thought for a few seconds that we had a connection though. It felt like she might tell me something." Lin made eye contact with Viv. "But she didn't."

"Nothing?" Viv asked. "What about her manner? The nonverbal stuff? Did you pick up on anything? Did she seem guilty? Did she seem shy? Remorseful? Angry?"

One corner of Lin's mouth turned up. "If you decide to sell the bookstore someday and make a career change, I suggest you look into becoming a prosecutor or an interrogator of some sort."

Viv made a face. "Did you know that nonverbal stuff makes up a majority of our communication with one another? It's not just what a person says that's the whole message."

Lin's face clouded. "You're right. When I think back on the conversation, nothing much stands out, but it unnerved me and I don't know why."

"Did you feel like Avery was hiding something?"

"I don't know." Lin had a feeling that Avery knew some things, but was holding that knowledge close. "She told me that she didn't steal the basket and that she didn't know who stole it."

"She could be lying about one of those things, or both of those things." Viv's expression revealed skepticism about the young woman.

"She also said she didn't think Martha would ever kill herself."

Viv sighed. "Avery's opinion about how Martha died is only an opinion. She doesn't know what was going on with the woman, what struggles she might have had. Just because Martha was hard-driving and full of herself doesn't mean that she could handle every stressor that came her way."

Lin sat quietly and then said in a soft voice, "*I* don't think Martha killed herself."

"I know that and you're probably right." Viv pushed her hair behind her ear. "But Avery doesn't have your skills and abilities. Avery might say anything just to get you off the right track. You can't trust her."

"She told me that I better watch my back."

Viv leaned back in her chair. "That I agree with."

"We have two things to consider." Lin sat up straighter. "Who stole the basket and who killed Martha?"

Viv gave a nod and took a sip from her glass. "Could be two different people or could be the same person."

"I'm voting that it's one person." Nicky came up to Lin and rubbed his head against her leg. "We need to think about motive."

"Why would someone kill Martha?" Viv asked. "We know she wasn't such a good person, but that isn't a reason for murder."

"Do you think she knew something about the theft? It could be that someone wanted her out of the picture so she wouldn't reveal what she knew. Maybe she saw something or overheard something."

# A Haunted Theft

"Could she have been a partner in the theft and then the partnership went bad?"

Lin's eyes widened. "That's an interesting idea. If she was a partner in the crime that could explain some of the things we overheard when we were outside Martha's office."

Viv looked pensive. "Do you think we should tell the police what we heard? They could pull the phone records and see who she was talking to at that time?"

"I think we should, especially with Martha dead. Things are escalating. Our information could help. Let's go tomorrow."

The girls went inside to the kitchen to start dinner. Viv announced what was in the fridge and they decided to make a shepherd's pie. Lin started to brown the beef in a frying pan while Viv peeled potatoes. The dog and cat sat near the stove in case any stray beef made its way to the floor.

Lin chuckled. "We can always count on these two to clean up anything that drops."

Viv agreed. "They always manage to show up when they think it's important."

Lin froze. Her hand holding the wooden spoon was suspended in mid-air. She turned slowly to face Viv.

When Viv saw the look on her cousin's face, she stopped peeling the potato she had in her hand. "What? What's wrong with you? Why do you have that look?"

"What you said." Lin removed the frying pan from the burner. "Just now."

Viv didn't know what she meant. "What did I say?"

"What you said about Nicky and Queenie. That they always show up when they think it's important."

Viv just stared. "So? They do."

Lin's heart was beating fast. "It made me think of something. The ghosts. They show up when they think it's important."

Viv cocked her head. "Yeah?"

"I saw the Wampanoag ghost twice. Where was I?"

"He showed up outside the cultural museum. Right after the theft."

"And the second time?" Lin smiled.

Viv's eyes brightened when she recalled the second time Lin had seen the ghost. "You saw him in the garden behind the cultural museum."

"Is it a message? Is he trying to tell me something?" Lin's voice trembled with excitement.

Viv's eyes widened. "It's not just because the theft happened at the museum. There must be a clue in there. That's why you've only seen him in that one place."

Lin nodded and the girls high-fived one another.

"And Sebastian," Lin said. "He showed up outside Lacey Frye's shop."

"Oh." Viv's mind raced. "What is he trying to

tell you? Is it something about Lacey? Is there something in her shop that could be a clue?"

"Or is he trying to tell me that there's something about Avery Holden? She lives behind Lacey's shop."

"This is progress." Viv smiled and returned to peeling the potatoes. "We're figuring things out." She placed the vegetables in the pot of boiling water and set the timer.

Lin finished browning the meat. "We need to go back to those two places."

"When are you starting the job on the cultural museum garden?"

"Soon. The exact day hasn't been worked out yet." Lin grinned, happy that she and Viv had made some progress understanding the ghosts' appearances.

They finished assembling the shepherd's pie and placed it in the oven. Viv poured two glasses of wine and they took their drinks out to the deck. The sun had set and shadows covered the back garden. The dog and cat nestled in the grass at the bottom of the deck steps.

Viv and Lin made plans to go out to a pub for dinner on the weekend with their boyfriends and they tried to figure out a day when the four of them could head for the beach for an afternoon of swimming in the ocean. Lin yawned. It was nice to sit and relax and think about other things besides a stolen item and a death.

Suddenly, Nicky leaped to his feet and let out a low woof. He scrambled up to the deck just as Queenie jumped onto the porch railing, arched her back, and hissed.

Lin sprang to her feet, her eyes flashing about the yard.

Viv hunched in her chair and pulled her sweater tight around her. "What is it?" Her voice shook.

The front doorbell rang and Viv vaulted out of her seat. "Now what?" She stared at her cousin.

Lin swallowed and gave a slight shrug of her shoulder. Her heart pounded like a drum had settled in her chest. Sucking in a deep breath, she said, "Let's go find out."

The girls walked through the house to the front door with the dog and cat racing ahead. Viv put her hand on the doorknob and hesitated. Lin nodded and Viv unlocked it and slowly opened the door a few inches.

A young woman's unsteady voice spoke. "It's me. Can I come in?"

Viv opened the door fully to reveal Mary Frye standing on the front porch under the light.

"Mary?" Lin's eyes were wide with surprise.

Mary slurred her words. "I ... I need to talk to you."

## CHAPTER 18

Viv stepped back to allow Mary to enter. The young woman stumbled inside, her ebony hair falling over her face, and Lin grabbed her arm to keep the girl from falling. Nicky and Queenie stared at the girl with concerned looks.

Lin mouthed to Viv, 'she's drunk.' Viv nodded and rolled her eyes as the smell of alcohol filled the air. They each held an arm and led Mary to the living room couch where she sprawled against the sofa back. Queenie and Nicky jumped into a chair next to the couch.

"Would you like some tea or coffee?" Viv eyed the girl.

Mary looked up at Viv with hooded eyes. "Hmmm?"

Lin nodded to Viv and then sat down sat next to Mary. "Viv's going to get you some tea."

Mary looked at Lin with teary eyes. "I need to talk to you." She rubbed at her lids.

"What's wrong?" Lin asked with a soft voice.

As Mary pushed herself up straighter and tried

to focus her bloodshot eyes, her body began to shiver and she pulled her light jacket tighter around her body. Lin reached for a throw blanket and placed it over the girl's shoulders.

"Did you come from a bar? Were you out with friends?" Lin tried to get Mary talking.

Mary shook her head and looked down at her hands. "I was alone."

"You had a few drinks?" Lin knew that was an understatement, but wanted to be tactful. "Where did you go?"

"A small pub in town."

"How did you know that Viv lived here?"

"I followed you one day." Mary tugged the blanket tighter over her shoulders.

Viv came in from the kitchen and placed a tray with tea mugs and cream and sugar onto the coffee table. Lin poured the hot liquid into a cup and added a bit of the cream before handing it to Mary. "Why don't you sip this?"

Mary took a gulp and wrapped her hands around the mug. Viv exchanged a look with her cousin.

"What would you like to tell us?" Lin tried again to get some information from the girl.

Mary blinked twice. Lin worried that the young woman's eyes were going to stay shut, but Mary gave herself a shake and lifted her gaze and moved her eyes from Viv to Lin. "I'm afraid." The words trembled in her throat.

The words sent a shiver along Lin's back. "What

are you afraid of?"

Mary looked around the room suspiciously as if she might find some danger lurking behind one of the chairs or the desk. "I'm not sure if I should say anything."

"Did someone threaten you?" Viv's eyes flashed with anger.

"I...." Mary began and then stopped.

"It's okay." Lin attempted to encourage the girl. She couldn't imagine what Mary had to say to them. "You can tell us. Does it have something to do with the museum?"

"In a way." Mary sucked in a deep breath. "I hope no one knows I came here." She looked like she might bolt off the sofa.

"It's dark out. I don't think anyone saw you come in." Although Viv wanted to be reassuring, she glanced at the big window of the living room and had the urge to get up and pull the curtains closed in case someone did see Mary come to the house.

"Who are you afraid of?" Lin put her hand on the girl's shoulder.

"Maybe I'm just blowing it out of proportion. Maybe I don't need to worry?"

Lin stifled a groan of exasperation. "Can you tell us what happened to make you feel worried?"

Mary took another sip of tea. "You know I work at the museum. I thought it would be a good part-time summer job. I major in history and thought it would be a good fit to be a volunteer so I could share my knowledge of the island. When I found out there was going to be a Lightship basket exhibition, I contacted Martha Hillman." Mary winced when she said the dead woman's name. "I can't believe she died. Martha accepted my offer to volunteer and after the first weeks, she decided to pay me. It was just a little money, but I was happy that Martha was pleased enough with my work there that she wanted to pay me." Mary pushed her hair back over her shoulder. "I teach the basket classes and work in my mother's shop sometimes. I have a little job at a coffee shop in town, too, just a few hours a week."

"You're busy." Lin smiled trying to be reassuring.

"I like to keep busy. I have a lot of energy. I'm super busy when I'm at school so I like to have different things to do in the summer." Sadness or worry pulled at the corners of Mary's mouth.

"How was Martha to work for?" Viv asked.

A muscle in Mary's cheek twitched. "She was okay."

"Okay?" Viv held Mary's eyes.

"Ms. Hillman was sort of mean. She was never very nice to anyone. Criticized people's work, was always correcting them. I tried to stay out of her way." Mary took a gulp from her mug. "At first, I thought that Ms. Hillman was so smart and hardworking and dedicated to the museum. She was all of those things, but she had an edge to her. People walked on eggshells around her."

"Did she frighten you?" Lin wondered if Mary's fear had to do with Martha, but dismissed the idea since Martha was dead. How could she cause Mary any worry now?

"I was always afraid I wasn't doing the right thing. She made me nervous."

"Is that what you wanted to tell us?" Viv asked. "That Martha scared you?"

"Yes. Well, no." Mary shook her head. "That was just part of it."

Although Lin wanted Mary to just come out and say what she needed to tell them, she knew that the girl had to reveal things in her own way.

"There was a woman who worked at the museum who I got along well with. She talked to me about other places she'd worked, where she'd gone to school and what she'd studied. She gave me advice." Mary screwed up her face. "Leading up to the basket exhibition, everyone got really busy. Tempers flared now and then. This woman seemed especially stressed out. I think Ms. Hillman was picking at her. I almost got the impression that she wanted this other woman to fail. Ms. Hillman seemed jealous or envious or something, almost like she hated her. I think she wanted a reason to get rid of her."

Lin asked even though she assumed who it was. "What was the woman's name?"

"Avery Holden."

"She got fired?"

"Yes. Ms. Hillman fired her. It was late one night. They were in Ms. Hillman's office. Everyone else was gone. The place was nearly dark. They were screaming at each other."

"Could you hear what they were saying?" Viv's eyes were wide.

"Just a word, here and there. I couldn't make sense of it."

"Can you remember any of the words you heard?" Lin wondered what might cause the two women to be shouting at one another.

Mary's face clouded. "They said something about the baskets. I heard them mention Nathan Long. Martha screamed something about how dare Avery do such a thing. I didn't understand what the argument was about. It didn't sound like the fight had anything to do with Avery's job performance." Mary shrugged. "Avery didn't come back to the museum after that."

Viv tilted her head to the side. "Why were you there so late?"

Mary swallowed and then spoke quickly. "After I'd left, I realized that I'd placed some of the historical instructional panels in the wrong sequence. I was afraid that Ms. Hillman would be angry. I decided to go back and see if the museum was still open. I thought some people might be working late since the exhibit opening was only a day away."

"The door was open?" Lin asked.

"The front door was locked, but there's a door at the rear that the employees use. It was open. I was so happy that the door was unlocked. I hurried inside. It was eerie in there. I didn't want to turn on any lights. The red security lights were on so I could see okay. I went to fix the displays. It only took a few minutes. Just as I was about to leave, I heard the screaming. It scared me. At first, I listened because I wondered if someone might need help. I don't know how long I stood there. I should have just rushed away."

"Did they see you in the museum when they were arguing?" Lin could see Mary's chest rising and falling.

"I went to the front door. You can exit even when it's locked. Just as I opened the door, Avery stormed out of Martha's office. Martha came out right on Avery's heels. We all made eye contact with each other and I flew out the door and down the steps."

"They didn't say anything to you?"

Mary shook her head.

"What about the next day? Or later in the week?"

"No. Avery is living in the studio apartment behind my mother's shop. We haven't spoken about that night. We avoid the subject. I don't see her much. At the museum, Ms. Hillman would glare at me, but she didn't say anything to me either about that night."

"So their fight scared you," Viv said.

"I'm feeling afraid." Mary's eyes filled up.

Lin's heart sped up. "Did you hear anything else that Avery and Martha were saying?"

"No." A tear slipped from Mary's eye and floated down her cheek.

Nicky jumped down off the chair and then leaped up on the sofa next to Mary where he snuggled against her. The young woman ran her hand over the dog's back.

"There's something else." Mary took quick looks at Viv and Lin. "When I was running down the steps of the museum, I smacked right into Nathan Long. He was coming up the steps toward me. I nearly screamed from surprise. I pushed away from him and darted down the street."

Viv said, "Nathan must have gone into the museum. He must have found out that Martha and Avery had a fight."

Lin leaned forward. "Did Nathan ever speak to you about that evening?"

Mary's face hardened. "He scares me. I hate him. The very next day ... he told me that it would be in my best interests if I forgot everything I heard and saw that night."

Lin's heart jumped into her throat.

## CHAPTER 19

Lin pulled up to Claire Rollins's house, let the dog out of the passenger side of the truck, and removed her tools from the back bed of the vehicle. She yawned as she and Nicky walked around to the rear of the property. It had been a late night and the alarm had gone off bright and early.

After their talk last night, Lin, Viv, and Nicky walked Mary Frye through Nantucket town to the door of her mother's shop. Lacey lived in the apartment on the second floor of the building and Mary wanted to go home and go to bed so that she could sober up.

On returning to Viv's house, Viv and Lin discussed what Mary had told them about the fight between Martha Hillman and Avery Holden and how she ran right into Nathan Long when hurrying out of the museum. Unable to reach any conclusions about who may have stolen the basket and who might have killed Martha, Lin left her cousin's house with Nicky and headed home to her cottage where she fell into bed exhausted from their attempts to determine the guilty party.

Claire was sitting on her deck holding a Bloody Mary and wearing a large straw hat and a pair of aviator frame sunglasses. "Oh, I forgot it was gardening day. Want a drink?"

Lin preferred to maintain professional relations with clients and thought it best not to become too friendly with them so she declined the offer of a beverage. "Thanks, but I need to keep on schedule today." She smiled and said breezily, "Lots to do."

Claire removed her legs from the deck chair they had been resting on and stood up. She stretched and then downed the liquid in her glass. "I could use another. I'll be a good girl and wait. But not too long." Claire's blonde curls were as bouncy as ever and they tumbled over her forehead as she made her way down the steps to the yard. "What are you doing in the garden today?"

Lin explained the work that was to be done in Claire's yard, all the while eyeing the young woman who seemed to have had more than one Bloody Mary already that morning. She noted how odd it was that she'd met two people in the past twelve hours who'd had too much to drink. Talking nonstop, Claire followed Lin around while she did her work.

At one point, Lin marveled at how the woman barely needed to come up for breath as she chattered on and on jumping from one topic to another without much encouragement at all. Lin grunted and "mm-hmmed" occasionally to convey some hints of interest, but realized quickly that Claire didn't need anything from her to keep rattling on.

Claire plopped down on the grass next to Nicky and stroked his fur. "Such a nice dog." She continued to run her hand over the dog's back. "Maybe I should get one."

"You like dogs?" Lin knelt by a bed and pulled weeds from between the flowers.

"I love them." Claire adjusted her glasses. "I suppose I'm too lazy to take care of one though."

"Do you work?" Lin thought that Claire wanted attention so she put effort into making conversation.

Claire snorted. She threw her head back and laughed. She took on the exaggerated tone of a haughty rich person. "My dear, I don't *work*." Claire let out a sigh. "People don't think I work, but putting on this front is a heck of a lot of effort."

Out of the corner of her eye, Lin glanced at the woman, and to be friendly, asked some questions about her life.

"I grew up in North Carolina. My father ran out on my mom when I was two. We never had two nickels to rub together, just dirt poor." Claire removed her hat and put it on the lawn next to her. "My poor mom worked so many jobs, lousy jobs, didn't pay squat. I decided when I was young that I wasn't going to poor ever again."

Lin moved to another part of the flower bed. "How did you meet your husband?"

"We met at his firm. I worked there. And no, I wasn't his secretary. I was a lawyer. We were in a meeting and I caught his attention."

"I didn't know that you are a lawyer." Lin pulled out some plants that weren't thriving.

"Was." Claire slipped onto her back and rested in the warm sun. "I hated that job. Thank God Teddy saved me from a life of misery."

"How long were you married?"

"A little less than two years." Claire shook her head. "I know people mock me for marrying someone so much older. They say I was only after his money. It wasn't that. Well, it was *partly* that, but I really cared for Teddy. He was kind to me."

Lin sat back on her heels and turned her head to her client wondering if Claire was revealing personal things because she'd been having drinks with breakfast.

"Now I'm alone."

"Do you have family?"

"I only had my mom. She died a few years ago, before I married Teddy." Claire's voice was mournful. "I bought her a small house. She was secure. But I never got the chance to show her what having lots of money felt like."

"Do you have friends who might like to visit you?"

"Believe it or not, I don't really have friends. I

have plenty of acquaintances from the boards I'm on, from the charities I'm involved with, but those people only associate with me because I have money."

Lin said, "That can't be the reason for everyone you know."

"Oh, it is. It's a funny crowd. Money makes their world go round. I play the game. We mingle and make pleasantries, but I honestly don't have a real friend." Claire kicked her shoes off and rubbed her toes in the grass. "Are you married?"

Lin shook her head.

"How old are you?" Claire looked at Lin.

"Twenty-nine." Lin pulled out some flowering annuals and dug new holes to replace them.

"I'm thirty-five." Claire sat up. "Do you have a boyfriend?"

"Yes. I just moved back here in June." Lin removed some impatiens from their little pots. "That's when I met him." Lin told Claire what Jeff did.

"Oh, he's a craftsman, someone who works with his hands. I admire that. I wish I had talent like that." Claire had a wistful expression on her face. "Did you get to see the antique basket? Before it was stolen?"

Lin sat on the grass. "I was at the exhibition the night it went missing."

"So you didn't see it?"

Lin gave a shake of her head.

A faraway look showed in Claire's eyes. "It was beautiful. I stood there for a long time and just stared at it. I imagined the person who made it. Moving the wood in and out. He or she must have been so proud of it." The woman ran her hand over the lush lawn. "It is believed the basket was made by a member of the Wampanoag tribe. You know they were in Massachusetts? Here on the island and on Martha's Vineyard?"

"Yes. In other parts of New England, too."

"You'll think I'm silly, but I'm sure that basket was made here."

"Why do you think that?" Lin eyed Claire.

"It's just a feeling I get." Claire's golden curls looked almost white in the direct sunlight. "It made me sad that the basket was in a museum off-island. It should be here. This is where it belongs."

Lin narrowed her eyes wondering if Claire might have wanted the basket to stay on Nantucket so badly that she stole it. "How do you think someone got it out of the museum? You're a board member. You're familiar with the layout of the place."

Claire didn't hesitate. "Anyone who knows the museum knew that the employee entrance was unlocked during operating hours. Hurry in, put it in a garbage bag, hurry outside with it like it's just filled with trash. It would have been easy. Do it right before the exhibition started the evening hours." She gave a shrug. "It's not rocket science."

Lin remembered the feeling of dread that had

come over her when she was in the basement of the museum with Nathan Long. "Is there a staircase from the basement up to the upper floor?"

"Yes. It goes up to the back of the building, right near the employee entrance. Why?"

"I wondered if someone might have taken the basket out through the basement. I didn't see a staircase when I was down there."

Claire looked surprised. "Why were you down there?"

Lin explained about being shown the basement when she'd been at the museum to give an estimate for the garden work. "Nathan told me the plans eventually called for a kitchen in the basement to serve the outdoor café."

A flash of something passed over Claire's face. "You were with Nathan, huh?" Her voice took on a hard edge. "Did he make a move on you when you were down there?"

Lin's eyes widened like saucers. "A move? No. God. Why would you say that?"

Claire pulled her knees up and hugged them. "No reason." Her tone softened.

"Claire, why did you ask that?" Lin asked.

"I'm just kidding. All the women love Nathan. He's very attractive. He's full of life." She put her sun hat back on. "I'm really hot. I think I need another drink." Claire stood up and started back to the house, but stopped and turned to Lin. "It was good talking to you." She hesitated for a moment, and then said, "Would you like to come by for dinner some night?"

Lin's immediate impulse was to make up an excuse, but she changed her mind. "Sure. That'd be nice."

Claire smiled and walked into the house. Lin watched her go.

When Claire talked about the antique basket, a strange feeling had come over Lin, one that she couldn't quite place. The sensation almost seemed to be a combination of loss and sadness, the very same feelings that she got from the Wampanoag ghost.

Nicky gave Lin's arm a nudge and she reached over to scratch his ears.

Lin wondered about what Claire had said about Nathan. Why did she ask if he'd made a move on her? She'd said that the women loved him and how he was so attractive. The comments made her feel unsettled for some reason. "What do you think, Nick?" She gave the little dog a hug and just as he licked her face, a wave of cold engulfed her.

Lin slowly raised her eyes to look over by the house. Sebastian Coffin stood staring at her.

In a moment, he disappeared.

## CHAPTER 20

The sun was setting when Viv helped Lin carry tools from the back of the truck to the yard space behind the cultural museum. She dropped them onto the ground and wiped her forehead. "Ugh. I don't know how you can work outside all day. The heat and humidity would kill me. Never mind the dirt and the bugs and the snakes.... ugh." She screwed up her face in distaste.

Lin laughed. "I know how you prefer the air conditioning, but look how strong I've gotten from all this work." She flexed her arm muscle.

Viv frowned. "You can keep your muscle. That's no incentive for me. I definitely made the right career choice."

On the way over to the museum, Lin had chattered away telling Viv about the conversation with Claire Rollins. "She seems lost and alone. She certainly didn't have an easy start to life with her father abandoning her and her mother. I can understand her drive to make something of herself."

"Well, she lucked out big time having Mr. Money-Bags fall for her. How come that never happened to me?"

"Claire honestly seemed to care for Teddy." Lin shook her head. "When she asked me that question about Nathan making a move on me, an awful feeling ran through my body. I think what she said about Nathan is some kind of a clue. What could it mean?" She glanced at her cousin sitting across from her in the passenger seat of the truck.

For the rest of the drive to the museum, the girls surmised what was going on and why Claire's comment could have made Lin so uneasy, and they came up empty.

"This space should be condemned." Viv scowled at the mess of a yard before them. "You've sure got your work cut out for you."

"At least now I can get started in the morning. There have been so many postponements with the board having to determine the funding source, the stolen basket hoopla, and Martha's death. I wasn't sure the contract was ever going to go through." Lin bent to pick up her tool box. She'd brought a length of heavy chain and a padlock to attach the tool box to an old metal fence post. With the teens sometimes using the space at night to hang out, Lin wanted to be sure her tools didn't disappear.

"You should ask Nathan to give you a key to the basement," Viv suggested. "Then you can store bigger tools inside. It's hard to get a parking space around here. With most of the tools already here, you could walk over to work sometimes instead of driving."

"Genius," Lin smiled. As she stood up holding the tool box in her hand, a feeling of dread washed over her. Her demeanor changed so rapidly that Viv immediately noticed the difference in her cousin.

"What's wrong with you?" Viv glanced around. "Is it a ghost?"

"No ghost." Lin dropped the box and hurried to the old metal table and chair where she sank onto the seat. "I got dizzy again."

Viv stood next to Lin and put her hand on her shoulder. "Is there some gas or something back here? Is some odor leaking out of that basement? Maybe a gas leak is making you feel odd when you're here."

"Then why doesn't it make *you* feel odd? Nathan didn't react to anything either when I was here with him. It's just me." Lin rubbed her temple. "No, I think it's something else that's making me feel weird."

"A clue?" Viv looked over her shoulders to be sure no one was sneaking up on them and then she muttered, "I should have stayed at the bookstore."

Lin took in some deep breaths trying to calm herself.

"Maybe you should give up this contract." Viv's voice quavered a bit. "Maybe it isn't safe for you to be around here."

Lin stood up, her hand resting on the tabletop. "I feel better. If there *is* a clue nearby, then there's no way I can give up this contract."

"Let's get out of here." Viv helped attach the tool box and other tools to the chain where they locked everything to the old fence on the other side of the yard. Heading back to the street, Viv suggested, "Leave the truck here. There won't be any place to park down near the pub."

"I was thinking the same thing. I can walk back this way to get the truck later tonight." The girls weaved along the streets of Nantucket town that led to the docks area. The streetlamps were just coming on and they shined like little beacons against the darkening sky. Entering the restaurant's lounge side, they miraculously found two stools at the bar.

Viv ordered a glass of wine and Lin asked for seltzer not wanting to drink any alcohol since her head still felt funny from being in the garden of the cultural museum. They enjoyed the music playing and the cheerful atmosphere of the place and they kept their chit-chat to topics other than a stolen basket and Martha Hillman's unexpected death.

Three men who were natives of the island and regular customers at Viv's bookstore-café approached the girls and struck up conversation. Lin judged them to be in the mid-sixties. Viv made introductions.

## A Haunted Theft

"We've seen you in the café sometimes. Viv tells us you run a landscaping business," the man named George remarked.

Lin told them about moving back to Nantucket and starting the new job and recently joining forces with Leonard Reed.

Harold said, "I know Leonard, haven't seen him for ages though. He's a good guy, a hard worker."

George's face lost its smile. "I always liked Leonard. We should give him a call. We lost touch years ago, right after his wife died." He shook his head sadly. "My wife and I were friends with Leonard and Marguerite."

Robert looked at Viv. "My wife told me she was in a basket class with you the other day. You took the class with Mary Frye? My wife raved about it."

Viv told them what she'd learned and how she wanted to take another class with Mary. "Funny, I never knew that Mary's mother owned the little basket shop in town."

"Oh, it's been there forever," Robert said. "Lacey's slowing down now though what with arthritis and other health problems. She looks ten years older than she is. Maybe her daughter will take over someday."

"You know Lacey?" Lin asked.

"Sure." Robert grinned. "You grow up on an island, you know most everyone."

George piped up. "Lacey hangs in there no matter what comes her way. She'll never stop weaving. Not while there's breath in her body."

"Yeah," Robert agreed. "She's a much better craftsperson than Nathan Long, but he gets all the fame and attention."

Harold said, "That guy is smooth. He knows how to work the business side of the baskets."

Robert narrowed his eyes. "My wife told me that Nathan learned the craft from Lacey. They dated back in the day. Lacey was a few years younger. They started a business together, and then Nathan cut her out. It was pretty nasty, I understand. He basically stole all Lacey's knowledge and set himself up as the great expert."

Lin and Viv's mouths dropped simultaneously.

Harold added, "Rumor was back then that Nathan took all the money he and Lacey had made together and left Lacey with nothing."

"That's horrible." Viv was shocked to hear such terrible things about the man she'd admired for so long.

"Shortly after that, Lacey left the island for a couple of years, she came back with a little daughter. A friend gave her space in the building she's in now to start over again. Lacey eventually bought the place."

"I never liked Nathan." George took a drink from his glass. "He was always a know-it-all, thought too much of himself. He could be a bully."

Robert added, "Couldn't deny his ambition. He had that in spades ... so much so that he didn't care who he hurt or trampled or took from to get what and where he wanted."

"You couldn't deny his charm or charisma either. That sure didn't hurt him," Harold said. "All the girls loved him. He was a real ladies man. Probably still is."

"Nathan's still a handsome guy." George motioned to the bartender for another round of drinks. "He must have a plastic surgeon on his staff because we haven't held up as well as he has."

The comment had the other men laughing.

Lin's head was spinning from the revelations about Nathan Long. Something about what the men were saying picked at her. An idea seemed to float into the edges of her mind, but when she tried to grasp it, the thought drifted out of reach.

The men moved on to other topics and chattered away, while Lin and Viv so shocked and surprised about Nathan Long, just nodded and murmured brief comments now and then. When their wives arrived to join them, the six said their goodbyes and headed for the dining room. Lin and Viv stared at one another.

"Well, that was unexpected information." Viv rolled her eyes and took a long drink of her wine. "I must be a terrible judge of character. I liked the guy. Jeez."

"You *are* a good judge." Lin leaned her elbows on the bar. "Nathan does have charm. Your interactions are minimal. You can't get a good idea about him in that short amount of time."

"So." Viv frowned. "Now what do you think?"

"I think someone has been overlooked." Lin ran her finger over her horseshoe necklace and leveled her eyes at her cousin. "And that someone is about to be put under a very large microscope."

"I can't wait." Viv raised her glass and clinked it against Lin's.

## CHAPTER 21

While Lin and Viv ate dinner at the bar, they talked over the new revelations and Viv stewed over what an awful person Nathan Long was and how foolish she was to be sucked in by his fame and charm.

The girls walked through town on their way home and split up at a fork in the road. The cousins hugged goodnight and Viv headed up the cobblestone streets to her house. Lin strolled the few blocks to pick up her truck that she'd left at the curb near the museum. Her head was still reeling with thoughts and ideas about the events of the past two weeks. She was happy to see that her vehicle was still where she left it and even though she knew she'd parked legally, she was afraid that it might have been towed away.

Taking out her keys, Lin reached for the driver's side door. Something caught her eye at the side of the museum. She thought she saw a flash or a flicker of light coming from behind the building and wondered if kids were back there and if they had tampered with her tools. Shoving her key into her pocket, Lin pulled out her phone so that she could place a call to the police if kids were indeed trespassing on the museum grounds.

Lin tiptoed along the side of the building as quietly as she could and peeked around the corner into the dark garden wishing that the board members had voted to pay for security lights for the property. Squinting into the darkness, Lin could see movement close to the area near the corner of the yard that had held evidence of teens congregating there.

Lin had to stifle a gasp of surprise. Someone was digging under the huge Beech tree. There was no one else in the garden, just the lone figure moving a shovel carefully into and out of the ground. *What in the world?* She took a step forward and her foot came down on a twig that snapped.

The figure whirled, dropped the shovel, and took off running around to the other side of the museum. Lin hesitated for a second and then hurried to see where the person went. Reaching the far corner of the building, she saw no one. Lin stood holding her breath trying to be as silent as possible, straining to hear for footsteps.

The clink-clunk of a bicycle chain sounded on the other side of the wooden fence that stood at the east side boundary of the museum's land. Lin rushed to the fence and stuck her face up to a crack in the wood just in time to see the figure racing away in the night.

Lin sighed and walked back to the section of the garden where she'd seen the person digging. Expecting to find a case of beer or some such thing being covered over with soil for a future teen gathering, Lin used the flashlight on her phone to light up the thing in the ground and poked at the object protruding from the earth. Bending down to get a better look, her breath caught in her throat as she fell back on her butt.

Wrapped in black plastic garbage bags, there was a small section of a handle sticking out. It was the stolen Wampanoag basket.

\*\*\*

Lin bustled in her kitchen putting breakfast dishes in the dishwasher and packing her lunch. She yawned as she reached for some water bottles and placed them in her canvas bag. Nicky sat watching his owner, his little tail wagging back and forth.

It had been a late night and she hadn't been able to sleep much. After discovering the antique basket in the shallow hole in back of the museum, Lin called the police, and then phoned Viv and Jeff who both raced to meet her.

The police asked a million questions, some more than once. When they asked about the figure that she'd seen digging, Lin couldn't tell them much.

"The person was on a bicycle and rushed away. I was looking through a hole in the fence, but it was dark and the hole was too small, and I didn't get a good look at all." Everything she said was true, but there was one thing that she kept to herself and she wasn't exactly sure why. Lin told herself that she couldn't be sure who was on that bike. Like she told the police officer, it was so dark outside. She didn't see the figure's face, but still….

Lin sighed feeling guilty for not being more forthcoming, but what if she was wrong about who it might be? She didn't want to falsely accuse someone.

Nicky barked and Lin jumped. She heard a car door shut and she went into the living room to look out the window. A black Range Rover was parked in front of her house. She hurried to the front door.

Lin smiled. "I thought that was your car." She opened the door.

Claire Rollins entered the little foyer. "Hi. Wow, what a great house." She admired the ceiling beams and the large windows and the bead board on the walls. "It's beautiful."

Lin gave a half smile knowing Claire was used to a whole lot more quality and space than what her cottage contained. "Claire, you don't have to go on and on. I appreciate it and all…."

"I mean it." The blonde gave Lin a serious look. "I'd love a house like this."

Nicky leaned against the woman's leg and she

bent to pat him. "You are the best dog ever." Nicky seemed to grow an inch taller from the praise.

"I hope you don't mind that I stopped by. I know it's early, but I thought you might be leaving soon for your jobs and I wanted to catch you."

"It's okay. My first job of the day got cancelled. I don't have to rush away." Lin couldn't start work on the museum garden until the investigation regarding the basket had been completed. Lin gestured to the sofa. "Want coffee or tea or something?"

Claire declined the offer and sat down. Lin took the chair across from her.

"Did you hear about the basket?" Lin wondered if Claire had heard the news.

"I did." A huge smile formed on her face. "I'm so glad it's been recovered. And there's no damage to it at all, thank heavens."

"Is that why you came by?" Although Lin's name hadn't been mentioned on the news, information often traveled quickly and Claire might have heard that Lin was the one who found the basket.

Claire looked surprised. "No." She folded her hands in her lap. "I wanted to talk about something else." Claire shifted her eyes from her hands to Lin. "You know, the other day when you were working in my yard? I was drunk, in case you hadn't noticed."

A smile crept over Lin's mouth.

Claire rolled her eyes. "I figured you'd noticed.

Anyway, I'd like to thank you. That was the first time in about two years that I talked to someone like a friend. Most everyone I talk to wants something from me. Oh, I know I pay you for the gardening and all, but you don't treat me like some queen, like I'm better than anyone else. You treat me normal."

"You're welcome." Lin chuckled. "You don't have to thank me for treating you like a normal person."

"Yeah, I do." Claire clasped and unclasped her hands.

Lin could see that the woman wanted to say something more.

After a few moments, Claire spoke. "I'd like to tell you something." She sucked in a long breath. "I asked you if Nathan Long made a move on you. Well, he made a move on me. I wondered how many other women he'd done that to." Claire shifted uncomfortably in her seat. "One day, I arrived early for a board meeting and Nathan was there already. He was all charming and sweet. Well, he got a little too close and touched my chest. I smacked him."

Lin couldn't help but give a little cheer. Claire's eyes widened and then she smiled. "I wanted to punch him in the nose actually."

"You should have." Lin told her some of the things she'd heard about Nathan Long from the men at the pub.

"I too was initially sucked in by his charm. He's horrid." Knowing that Lin was on her side, Claire relaxed and leaned back in her chair. "I told Martha Hillman what he'd done. I thought Nathan should be disciplined by the board, maybe kicked off of it. You know what Martha said? I must have misinterpreted Nathan's actions."

Lin's jaw dropped.

"Yup. She berated *me*. She said I must have led him on. Can you imagine? In this day and age? She blamed *me*. I wanted to kill her." Claire's eyes widened and she stammered. "I mean, I wouldn't, I didn't...."

Lin nodded. "I know what you mean."

"I need to tell you something else. Two things, actually." Claire hesitated again, but then went on. "I think Nathan and Martha had a thing. Well, I'm sure of it. I saw them one night."

Lin sat up straight.

"I saw them in Martha's office. They didn't know I was still there. They were kissing. Passionately. I walked backwards as quietly as I could and then I practically ran from the place."

Lin's heart pounded. "They didn't know that you saw them?."

"No. I've been wondering." Claire lowered her voice even though they were the only ones in the house. "Do you think Nathan could have killed Martha? You know, a lover's quarrel gone wrong? I can't stop worrying about it."

"I guess it's certainly possible." Lin's head was spinning from this news.

"I hate to be a gossip, but in light of everything, I felt like I had to tell someone. I don't have anyone else I can talk to about it. Do you think I should tell the police?" The corners of Claire's green eyes wrinkled with worry.

"Maybe." Lin nodded. "Maybe you should, yes. You said you had two things to tell me?"

Claire bit her lip. "I saw something else. I went to the museum early one morning to pick up some folders. As I passed Nathan's office, I saw him. He was trying to kiss someone. The person was squirming to get away. I stopped in the doorway and shouted at him. The girl ran past me and Nathan glared at me. I gave him a piece of my mind. You know what he said? The girl was consenting and I'd better stay out if it." Claire's eyes narrowed. "That girl was *not* consenting."

"What did you say to him when he told you to stay out of it?" Lin asked.

"I told him I had enough money at my disposal to bring him down and that if I ever saw him do anything to that girl again or anyone else, for that matter, then he would rue the day he crossed me."

Lin applauded.

"I talk big, but I was ready to faint. He scared me, Lin. I'm still afraid of him."

"Keep away from him. Don't ever be alone with him." Lin's expression was serious.

## A Haunted Theft

Claire nodded. "I tried to talk to the girl one day about what had happened. She wouldn't acknowledge what I'd seen."

"Do you mind if I ask who the girl was?"

"Mary Frye."

Anxiety washed over Lin like a ten foot wave.

## CHAPTER 22

The mid-day sun was hot and bright when Lin approached Lacey Frye's shop. She stood outside before plucking up her courage to go in. Just as she was about to reach for the doorknob, the click-clack of a bicycle chain made her turn around.

Mary stopped her bike on the street and when she noticed Lin on the porch of the shop, a look of panic spread over her face. Lin was afraid the young woman would speed away, but Mary swung her leg over the seat of the bike, took in a deep breath, and faced Lin.

"Are you looking for me?" Mary walked the bike closer to the porch steps.

Lin nodded. "Can you talk?"

"Why don't we walk down to the docks," Mary suggested. She parked the bicycle on the right side of the store building and locked it to the small fence.

The two walked along the brick sidewalks together.

"What were you doing last night?' Lin thought

# A Haunted Theft

the question was vague enough not to be accusatory.

"I was out."

"Where did you go?"

"A few places."

Lin said, "I went by the cultural museum last night. I left my truck parked out front. I went back to get it and thought I saw a flash of light behind the building so I walked around to the garden." Lin paused to see if Mary might say something.

When they reached a park bench positioned near the beginning of the docks, they sat down side by side.

Lin continued. "Someone was in the backyard. It looked like the person was digging. I frightened her and she ran away. I heard the sound of a bike chain so I knew the person rode away and there was no use chasing after."

"Then what happened?" Mary watched the sails bobbing in the harbor.

"I went back to where the person had been digging. There was a hole. I found the stolen basket and then called the police."

Mary turned her head to Lin. "Were you able to describe the person to the police?"

Lin pushed away a strand of hair that blew into her eyes. "It was very dark. The person was wearing black, had a hat on. I couldn't tell the police much." Lin felt Mary relax slightly. "You know how people have a distinct walk or way of moving? Like if you're in a dark corridor, you can often tell who the person is, if you know them, who is coming towards you? It's nothing that really stands out, but the way someone moves or walks can almost seem as unique as a fingerprint." Lin faced Mary. "You know what I mean?"

Mary didn't say a word for almost a full minute. "I was at the museum late one night. We had duties like clean-up and keeping the place neat. There wasn't enough money to hire a custodian, so we all pitched in. I could hear Nathan Long talking to someone in his office. At first, I thought he was on the phone, but then I could hear a woman's voice. She was speaking low. I couldn't make out who it was. I started to move away from the door when what they were talking about made me freeze in my tracks."

Mary gave Lin a quick look. "They were making plans to steal the antique basket." Mary sucked in a breath. "I couldn't believe it. I inched closer to the door to try and hear more clearly. Their plan was to keep the employee door unlocked right before the evening exhibition hours started. Right before most of the employees came in, they would bring a trash can through the exhibition rooms, take the basket off the pedestal and put it in the trash can. Wheel it to the closet. There's an old dumbwaiter in the side closet. They'd hide it there until after hours. Leaving the employee door unlocked would spread suspicion that someone came in from outside and took the basket."

"Could you make out who Nathan was talking to?"

"No, the woman spoke too low, she was whispering. Sometimes I didn't even know she had said anything, but Nathan would answer so I knew she was talking." Mary put her elbows on her knees and leaned forward. "They planned to sell the basket through an underground art and artifacts dealer network. The theft was planned for the night *after* the basket actually went missing."

"You removed it?" Lin wondered how Mary would react to her question.

Mary snorted. "They had the whole thing worked out. I heard the whole plan so I enacted it myself. Just one day early." Mary sat up, a look of anger on her face. "I wasn't going to let them steal that basket." She shook her head. "No. They weren't getting their hands on it."

"Why didn't you just go to the police and tell them what you heard?" Lin asked.

Mary cocked her head. "A twenty-two-year-old nobody reports overhearing a plot to steal an antique basket and the thief happens to be a world-renowned craftsman, author, and lecturer. The twenty-two-year-old has no proof. What do you think would have happened? Would the police believe me or Nathan Long?" Mary's eyes flashed. "Nathan Long was *not* going to steal that basket."

Lin blew out a long sigh. "What were you going

to do with the basket?"

"I knew you'd find it when you started the garden renovations. I didn't have to do anything."

"Why were you digging it up then?" Lin looked at Mary with narrowed eyes.

"I heard Nathan and some other board members arguing about the cost of doing the garden. They wanted to postpone things due to the theft of the basket. They were afraid the museum would have to be closed because of the insurance payout that would have to be paid to the lending museum for the loss of the basket. I couldn't leave the basket buried for long. It would have been damaged. I decided to dig it up and leave it at the police station."

Lin believed every word of what Mary had just told her. "Who do you think was Nathan's accomplice?"

"I've been trying to figure that out." Mary leaned back against the bench. "I can't stop thinking about it."

"Martha Hillman?"

"Maybe. I'm not sure."

"Another one of the board members?" Claire Rollins popped into Lin's mind. Ideas sparked like lightning. *Did Claire make things up about Nathan Long to divert attention from her alliance with him?* Lin's heart sank. *But why would Claire take the chance stealing the basket with him? She didn't need the money.* Another thought pushed its way into Lin's brain. *Claire was lonely and alone. Maybe she'd fallen for Nathan's charms.*

Lin wanted to test what Claire had told her. She turned to Mary. "I've heard that Nathan Long was a ladies' man. Did you ever see him flirting with staff?"

Mary's jaw set and the muscles of her face tightened. "Sure. He thought he was hot stuff. He acted all nice and friendly with all of the women. Complimenting them, smiling, joking, putting his hand on theirs. It would have been easy for people to get the wrong impression, think he was interested in them."

"Were any of the women particularly taken with Nathan? I wonder if someone like that might be talked into helping him steal the basket."

"I don't know." Mary bit her lip, hesitated for a few moments, and then blurted, "Once I saw Martha Hillman and Nathan kissing in the storage area in the basement. I was taking the trash outside. I saw them through the window."

"Nathan and Martha." Lin's eyes flashed. "Do you know that the police think that Martha may have been killed?"

"Killed?" Mary looked stunned. "Martha killed herself. It was suicide."

"It seems that it might not have been suicide."

"What?" Mary was on the edge of her seat. "It might be murder?" She ran her hand through her hair. "I wondered if Martha and Nathan hatched the plan to steal the basket together. I wondered if the two of them broke off with each other because their plan failed." Mary stared at Lin red-faced. "Did I cause her death? I removed the basket so they couldn't steal it. Did Nathan go into a rage and kill Martha because their plan derailed?" She clutched the sides of her head. "Is she dead because of what I did?"

Lin gripped Mary's shoulder and spoke firmly. "Nothing you did caused this. If someone killed Martha or she killed herself ... it's not your fault. It's not."

Tears gathered in the corners of Mary's eyes and her hands were trembling. "My God, did Nathan commit murder? I thought he loved Martha. How could he do that?"

"Maybe the only one Nathan loves is himself," Lin muttered.

"He's a monster." Mary nearly choked on the words.

Lin spoke to Mary with a gentle tone. "I have to ask you a question. Did Nathan ever do anything inappropriate with you?"

Mary's eyes widened. "What do you mean?" Her voice quavered.

"Did he ever try to kiss you?"

"No." Mary's eyes flashed. "He did not." She stood abruptly. "I need to get to the museum. I'm working later." She took a step and then wheeled on Lin. "Are you going to tell the police I buried the basket?"

"I didn't see your face last night. I think the person who knows what happened should be the one who tells the police." Lin held Mary's eyes. "That doesn't mean I won't tell them one day if someone else doesn't."

Mary strode away leaving Lin sitting alone on the bench thinking. *Did Claire lie to me about Nathan? Who was the woman Nathan was plotting to steal the basket with? Who killed Martha?*

Lin felt like her head was about to explode.

## CHAPTER 23

Lin returned to her jobs more confused than at any point in the case. While working in her clients' yards, she kept looking over her shoulder hoping that a ghost would appear and steer her in the right direction, but no spirits showed themselves. Lin needed to catch up on some gardening tasks and by 6pm, she was dirty and exhausted and frustrated.

All the time she was pulling weeds, mowing, and planting, her mind was working on all the clues, motives, and suspects that she'd been able to come up with and the whole thing was still a jumbled mess. She pulled out her phone to call Libby about getting together to talk over everything and she sighed before sending the call, remembering that the older woman had gone off-island for a few days.

Still holding the phone, it buzzed with an incoming text from Viv reminding Lin that they were taking the second basket weaving class with Mary. There was a change in location. The class was being held at the cultural museum.

Lin wiped her soil-covered hand on her shorts

and then rubbed her forehead. There was no way she was going to that class. Lin looked down at her dog. "What's going on, Nick? Will we ever figure it out?"

Lin wanted to talk to Viv, or Leonard, or Libby. She also wanted to talk to Jeff and wished he knew that she could see ghosts. That was a discussion she'd put off, waiting until they knew each other better. She knew she'd have to tell him soon and was dreading his reaction, afraid that she would lose him. Lin wanted to collapse onto the grass and fall asleep to escape from all the confusion. Instead, she picked up her tools and dragged herself to the truck with Nicky following behind.

Just as she slammed the truck bed, Leonard pulled up beside her. She was so happy to see him, she almost cried. Nicky bounced and twirled with delight that Leonard was there.

"What's wrong with you, Coffin?" Leonard narrowed his eyes.

"I'm tired."

Leonard leaned out his window. "You're always tired. It's more than that. What's going on?" He got out of the truck and leaned down to scratch Nicky's ears.

"A lot. A lot's going on. Want to hear it?"

"Yeah. Can you talk fast? I'm taking the 7:30 ferry to the mainland."

A wave of panic shot through Lin's body. "How long are you going to be gone?"

"I'm taking the last ferry back tonight. I'm going to see a piece of equipment that we could use. We can get it at a good price. It's practically a steal. I'll text you a picture of it if it's as good as I think it is."

"Okay." Lin nodded and tried to figure out why she was feeling a sense of being abandoned. She knew it was nonsense to think such a thing and she sucked in a deep breath to try and shake it off.

"I thought you'd be excited about the equipment."

"I am. It's great." Lin forced a smile. "You want to get some take-out before you go?"

Leonard eyed his partner trying to figure out why she seemed so off. "Yeah. Let's go."

Nicky rode with Leonard to the farm where he bought chicken sandwiches and boxes of french fries and onion rings and met Lin back at her house. They took the food to the deck and Lin started a whirlwind of chatter telling Leonard all the things that she'd discovered in the past few days ... leaving out the ghost stuff.

Leonard stared at Lin. "So Martha was probably murdered. I despised that woman, but all I can feel is sorrow." He put his sandwich on his plate.

Lin gave a nod of understanding.

Leonard said, "And Mary Frye removed the basket to keep it from being stolen. Good for her, even though she's bound to get into a heap of trouble over it."

"She should have told someone what she heard

Nathan and the unknown woman discussing. Maybe she could have gotten help. She took the basket without thinking it through. She could have avoided getting herself into trouble." Lin held her cold glass of seltzer against her temple.

Leonard took a drink of his beer. "Speaking of trouble, it seems that Nathan Long is causing a lot of it." He scowled. "Nothing sticks to that guy. He sets up a plot to steal the basket, he thinks all the women are in love with him, he manipulates people to help him commit a robbery. I wonder what else he's done that no one knows about." Leonard checked his watch. "I gotta get going or I'll miss the ferry. Try to stay out of trouble until I get back, okay?"

"Okay." Lin smiled and walked Leonard to the door. She gave him a hug, thankful to have him as a friend. "Thanks. I feel better."

The big man gave the dog another pat and then drove away with a wave.

Lin cleared the deck table of the dinner things and then she went inside and collapsed onto the sofa. Before she nodded off, she sent Viv a text telling her cousin that she wouldn't be able to make the basket class.

*\*\**

Lin bolted up, disoriented from her brief nap. Her sleep had been restless and full of crazy dreams that wove all the clues into a frightening tapestry of wild images and dark colors. She pushed herself up from the sofa and went into the kitchen to splash cool water on her face. Drying her cheeks on a towel, something popped into Lin's mind with such force that she felt like she'd touched a live electrical wire.

Lin ran to her front door. Nicky stood in front of it barking at his owner as if he was trying to make her stay in the house.

Lin side-stepped the dog, rushed out of the house, and took off running into town.

\*\*\*

Lin knocked on the door of the second floor apartment and just when she thought that no one would answer, it opened a crack.

"It's me, Lin Coffin. Can I talk to you?"

The door shut for a moment, a chain was pushed to the side, and then the door opened wide. Lacey Frye stepped back to let Lin enter. Lin didn't know why, but when she woke from her nap, she felt the urgent need to talk to Lacey and knew that she couldn't delay.

The cozy living room had a fireplace on one wall with pictures of Lacey and Mary in silver frames lining the mantle. Two upholstered chairs flanked the fireplace and a big, soft sofa stood facing it. Lamplight glowed and warmed the space. The two women sat in the chairs.

Lin didn't know where to start so she blurted out the question that was foremost in her mind. "Did Mary tell you about the basket?"

Lacey nodded. "Yes. She told me what she did. I'm afraid of what will happen to her when the authorities find out."

"Can you tell me why you hate Nathan Long?" Lin didn't know the question was going to come out of her mouth until she'd said it.

Mary blinked several times. Her facial expression revealed the inner turmoil of deciding whether or not to give Lin an answer. Finally she said, "I'll tell you. Nathan and I lived together for a number of years. We started a basket business together. I taught him everything I knew and then he left me. He took all the money we had made together. He went on to fame and fortune. I realized that he never loved me. He stole from me ... my knowledge, our money, my love. He left me with nothing."

Lin made eye contact with the woman who had lost so much at the hands of a man who only cared about himself.

Lacey glanced down at her hands clasped together on her lap. "I hate Nathan, yes, and I'm ashamed that I fell for his lies. I wanted to believe he loved me, that we were partners." She looked up at Lin. Her eyes had softened. "He didn't leave me with nothing. He left me with the best part of my life."

Lin realized what Lacey was telling her. "Mary."

Lacey nodded. "Mary is Nathan's daughter."

"Does she know?"

"Yes." Lacey sighed. "She found a long-ago letter from Nathan to me. She figured it out just a few months ago."

"Does Nathan know that he's Mary's father?"

Mary's face hardened. "No. And he never will."

The two sat quietly for several minutes.

Lacey broke the silence. "Mary told me that you said that Martha Hillman may not have committed suicide. Do you think Nathan killed her?"

Lin shook her head. "I don't know. If he didn't do it with his own hands, I think he's the reason she's dead."

Lacey gave a nod. "Martha was in love with Nathan her whole life. Mary saw them kissing recently. I don't believe Nathan ever loved the woman, maybe he doesn't know how to love. I think he used her like he's used everyone else. I think Martha was the one that Mary heard plotting with Nathan to steal the basket." Lacey paused, and when she spoke her voice was tight. "Nathan kissed Mary once. That monster. He called her into his office and...." Lacey's face flushed with anger.

What Claire had told Lin was true. While Lin's stomach clenched with disgust at Nathan Long, her body flooded with relief that Claire hadn't lied to her.

Lacey said, "You know, there were many times when I wanted to kill Nathan with my bare hands, but the kindness and love of my friends … those things saved me. When Nathan deserted me, I went to stay with a friend on the mainland. I stayed with her for three years and finally felt alive again. I took Mary back here, we came home. Another friend owned this building and gave me the shop downstairs for free to start my business. Eventually, I bought the building from her. Without those two friends I don't know where I'd be. I've tried to help other women over the years. It's my way of paying back. I have a woman downstairs now. She lost her job at the museum. Mary told me about her. We offered the studio apartment to her for free to help her out."

Lin's brain zinged. "Avery."

Lacey nodded.

The word repeated in Lin's head. Avery. Avery. *I won't tell you why Martha fired me. Watch your back. Some people aren't what they seem.*

Lin's heart pounded. *Avery was warning me about Nathan.* She leapt to her feet. "Do you know if Avery is in her apartment?"

"She isn't," Lacey said. "She gave me the key. She's leaving tonight on the late ferry. She's moving back to the mainland."

*Oh, no. Is Avery going to try and hurt Nathan?*

Some of the puzzle pieces had fallen into place.

## CHAPTER 24

Lin took off running from Lacey's apartment. She yanked her phone out of her pocket and placed a call to Viv. The phone rang and rang until Viv's voicemail came on. Lin called again and got the voicemail a second time causing her to curse. She yelled a message into the phone. "Viv, if you're still at the museum, get out of that building. Now."

Lin ran as fast as she could. The class had to be over. Viv must have left already. *Please let the class be over.*

Avery Holden had been fired. She and Martha had argued so fiercely that Mary Frye had been frightened by it. Nathan Long told Mary to forget what she'd seen and heard.

Lin feared that Avery Holden had been romantically involved with Nathan and that Martha and Avery found out that they were both in a relationship with Nathan. *Was Avery on the way to the museum to get revenge on Nathan before leaving on the last ferry to the mainland?*

As Lin approached the museum, she could see

that all the windows were dark. Breathing hard and trying to catch her breath, Lin moved around the building trying to see if there was any light on in any of the rooms.

Moving into the rear garden, she almost missed it. There was light at the back of the basement and she could see several shadows moving about. Lin crept to the basement door and took out the key she'd received in order to store her tools in the basement. She turned the handle. It clicked and she froze, afraid that whoever was inside had heard it. Lin crouched down and waited.

After a minute passed and no one came to investigate the noise, she crawled into the cellar on her hands and knees so no one would see her moving about. Shuffling silently to the back room, she could hear a woman's voice. Lin slid across the floor to hug the wall and inched closer to the open door of the back room.

Nathan Long spoke, fury dripping from his words. "You were at Martha's house. You saw me."

"I didn't. I wasn't there," Mary Frye cried. "I don't know what you're talking about."

Lin didn't know what to do. Her legs trembled and her body flooded with fear. She stayed in her crouched position, waiting.

"You saw me. You saw what I did." The man's voice cracked with anger.

Still on her hands and knees, Lin shifted an inch closer to the doorway and peeked inside. Nathan

Long, his back to her, was holding a gun on Mary. Lin's heart dropped. Viv was standing next to Mary with her arm around the young woman's shoulders.

Lin was just about to rush into the room when she saw Avery Holden appear behind Mary and Viv. She walked with purpose and stood in front of the two young women. Avery glared at Nathan. "You've ruined so many lives. You get away with it every time. You aren't getting away with it this time."

She took a step forward. "I thought you loved me." Avery's voice dripped with venom. "You used me. You told me to keep the employee entrance unlocked during the exhibition. You were going to steal the basket and frame me by telling the police I deliberately kept the door unlocked so I could steal it." Avery shook her head. "You and Martha were working together. Martha told me that unless I left the museum and kept my mouth shut, she would tell the police I was the one planning the robbery." Avery sneered. "I told Martha that you and I were involved. That's why she turned on you. I followed you that night ... the night you went to Martha's house. It was me, not Mary, who saw you. I looked in the window. Martha was already dead. I saw you carrying her away to the garage."

Nathan's shoulders were rising and falling with rage.

Lin wished Avery would stop talking. She was sure that Nathan was only moments away from shooting the three of them. What to do? What to do? Lin's brain was racing so fast she couldn't think straight. She wouldn't let anything happen to Viv. She had to take the chance.

Just as Lin rose to her feet and burst into the room, her phone rang. The combination of her rushing forward and the noise of the phone startled Nathan and he wheeled around to face Lin.

Before Nathan knew what was happening, Avery, Mary, and Viv were on him wrestling him to the floor. The gun dropped from Nathan's hand and Lin kicked it across the room. Avery removed her belt and tied Nathan's hands behind his back. Kneeling on the man's back, she said in between gasps for breath, "Who wants to call the police?"

With tears of relief running down her face, Lin hurried to Viv and held out her hand to help her cousin up off the floor. They stared at each other for a moment, and then wrapped their arms around one another in a hug.

Lin's phone rang again.

Viv looked at her cousin with a wan smile. "You better answer it."

Lin removed the phone from her pocket. The call was from Leonard. It went to her voicemail. She listened.

Leonard's voice sounded frantic. "Wherever you are and whatever you're doing, get out. I think you're in danger."

The corner of Lin's mouth went up. She sent her partner a text. *Thanks for the warning.*

*Everything's okay.*

## CHAPTER 25

The sun was nearly to the horizon and streaks of pink and blue and violet painted the sky. Lin, Jeff, Viv, John, Leonard, and Anton sat in the deck chairs of John's boat sipping drinks and watching the tourists stroll by on the docks. Nicky and Queenie rested on the deck listening to the humans chatter.

When the guys went below to check on the food, Lin stopped Leonard before he went below. "Thanks again for calling me with the warning. You have really strong intuition."

Leonard shrugged a shoulder. "It was just a feeling. I thought I should tell you." He hurried down the steps to the galley. Leonard didn't like the odd sensation he often got when Lin was in danger and he always tried to minimize it.

Viv leaned towards Lin. "There's something I don't get. In the past, when what the ghosts have wanted is resolved, then they appear to you like they're thanking you for having helped. The Wampanoag ghost hasn't shown up. We took down

Nathan Long. The basket has been found. Why hasn't he shown up?"

Lin looked out over the dark blue water. "I've been wondering that very same thing. Now I think that the ghost was concerned over two things, the basket being recovered and Mary Frye being safe from Nathan." Lin whispered. "I've been wondering if the ghost is a long-ago relative of Mary and Lacey."

"Oh." Viv sat up. "That makes sense." A faraway look passed over her face. "How lovely, to have someone from long ago watching over you."

Lin smiled. "It's also lovely to have someone from *now* watching over us." She thought of all the people in her life she could count on for help.

The guys could be heard coming up the steps with the food. Lin and Viv arranged the chairs around the deck table and everyone settled and dug into the meal. Discussion turned to Nathan Long.

John said, "My friend at the police station told me that the police were close to arresting Nathan Long for the murder of Martha Hillman. A warrant for his arrest was going out the morning after all of you attacked him."

Viv's voice was harsh. "We were defending ourselves from a monster."

Lengthy news articles and stories had been focusing on the events of the past weeks and most of the things that Lin and Viv had uncovered were now widely known.

"I can't believe that guy. What arrogance." Jeff shook his head. "He wanted that antique basket for himself but enlists Martha to help him by making her think he cares about her and that they would sell the basket on the underground market and share the money."

"Nathan Long pretended to care about the history and craftsmanship of the baskets." Viv's brow creased in anger. "All he cared about was the fame and money the craft could bring him."

"What a sociopath," Anton shook his head slowly. "The man had no empathy for anyone. I know that Martha Hillman was an awful person, but she didn't deserve to have her life ended by that terrible man. When I think back on all of the interactions I had with Nathan over the years ... and I never picked up on anything."

"It's hard to know a person, Anton," Lin observed. "Some people are masters of hiding their true selves and presenting a front to the world."

"So Martha was going to help Nathan steal the basket." John reached for the platter of grilled chicken. "She must have been shocked to discover the basket missing the day before she and Nathan were going to steal it."

Anton looked at Lin. "It was no act when she came over to us distraught that the basket was gone."

Lin nodded. "Things were not going as Martha had planned. The basket disappeared before she and Nathan could steal it and then Avery tells Martha that she is romantically involved with Nathan. Martha's plans were blowing up all around her."

Viv added, "Avery figured out that Martha and Nathan were involved with each other. Nathan told Avery not to lock the back door during the exhibition hours. Nathan and Martha would steal the basket and then tell the police that they'd discovered that Avery wasn't locking the back door because *she* must have stolen the basket. Suspicion would be put on Avery. After the police investigated, they wouldn't be able to pin anything on her, but Avery's career in museums would be over. No one would trust her. She would never get hired again."

Leonard piped up. "And Nathan would have dumped Avery and Martha, probably would have sold the basket, put the money away, and gone on to the next thing that he wanted."

"Nathan probably planned to kill Martha all along." Jeff sighed. "Otherwise she would have gone straight to the police after they stole the basket and he dumped her."

John said, "Unless Nathan made everything look like Martha stole it on her own. Nathan would sell the basket on the underground market and it wouldn't be recovered. I bet Nathan had it all planned how he'd get Martha into trouble. Maybe say she and Avery were in on it together."

## A Haunted Theft

Lin filled her glass with seltzer. "Mary Frye got sucked into it because she overheard Nathan and Martha planning everything." She glanced over at Viv. Viv was the only person she'd told about Nathan being Mary's father and neither one would ever tell another soul. "When Viv and I were outside Martha's office and overheard her phone conversation, Martha must have said to get "her" off the island, meaning Avery. Martha was probably concerned that Avery would go to the police with her suspicions."

Viv set her fork down and dabbed her lips with her napkin. "Avery was clever to send an email to the police telling them everything she knew about Nathan and that she'd seen him carrying Martha's body into the garage to make it look like suicide. She sent the email right before she went to the museum to confront Nathan. She wanted him to know that his evil deeds were about to catch up to him and that she'd had a hand in bringing him down."

"She could easily have been killed," John said. "Nathan might have shot her."

Viv sucked in a deep breath. "I don't think she thought he would be armed. Thank heavens Avery showed up looking for him. I stayed late at the class with Mary. Nathan came in and he forced both of us into the basement." She looked over at Lin and Leonard. "And thank heavens that my cousin showed up, too. Leonard's call came in right as Lin rushed into the room. The unexpectedness of those two things threw Nathan off just long enough for us to attack him." Viv smiled and flexed her muscle. "And I must say, it felt pretty good taking him down."

Lin chuckled. "I guess moving crates of books around your store develops as many muscles as outdoor gardening and landscaping does. You *did* make the right career choice."

After dessert and another hour of sitting on the boat deck in the cool, clear evening air, the little party broke up and everyone headed home. With the streetlamps lighting the way, Lin and Jeff walked hand in hand through town with Nicky trotting after them. All the way to her cottage, Lin thought about how lucky she was to have such wonderful friends and such a unique skill as being able to see the ones who have passed.

She thought about Lacey Frye's friends and how they helped her get back on her feet when she'd lost everything and had a tiny daughter to take care of.

Jeff squeezed Lin's hand as they turned down her street. It filled Lin's heart with warmth and then caused a pang of regret to wash over her. She didn't want to keep secrets from him anymore, but thinking of telling him about the ghosts nearly caused her to be sick. She was sure he would leave her.

Approaching the cottage, they saw a black Range Rover parked in front of Lin's house. Nicky woofed and wagged his little tail.

"Who's that?' Jeff asked.

"It looks like Claire Rollins's car."

Claire's white-blonde curls sparkled in the moonlight. She looked up as Jeff and Lin came up to the house. A big smile spread over the woman's face. "I was just going to write you a note." She waved a piece of note paper and a pencil in the air.

Lin made introductions and Jeff went inside to put tea on.

"Everything worked out." Claire's eyes were happy. "Nathan Long got arrested and the basket has been recovered."

Lin nodded. "Why were you leaving a note?"

"I'm moving."

Lin's heart dropped. "To where?"

"I'm moving to Boston. I'm selling the house. I know your friend, John, is a Realtor. I'm going to give him the listing." She winked. "He'll make a bundle on it."

"Why? Why are you going?" Lin wanted Claire to stay. She'd hoped that they would become good friends.

"I need a change. Everything here reminds me of Teddy. People think I'm a gold-digger." She shrugged and gave Lin a big smile. "I feel like making my own mark on the world."

"Well, do it here."

"I think I can make a bigger impact in other places." Claire stepped forward and hugged Lin.

"Thank you for being kind to me, for treating me like a friend. It meant a lot."

Lin frowned. "You are a friend. I wish you were staying. Keep in touch, will you?"

Claire squeezed Lin's hand. "You bet I will." She headed to her car.

"Hey. We were supposed to have dinner."

Claire laughed. "I'm only in Boston. It's not that far away, you know."

As she watched Claire drive away, Lin's phone rang in her pocket. "Anton? Hi."

"Lin. I'm so excited. Someone is making a deal with the Prentiss Museum to purchase the antique basket. The deal is almost finalized and the basket will be going to the Nantucket Historical Museum. It's going to stay on the island."

Lin's heart nearly jumped from her chest. "What? That's wonderful. Who is the donor?"

"Anonymous. It's a fabulous gift for the island. Oh, and I've also heard that Mary Frye won't be charged by the police for hiding the basket. I must call Libby now. I wanted to let you know. " Anton clicked off.

Still holding her phone, Lin looked up the road where Claire had just driven away. Lin smiled. *Claire.*

Claire believed that the basket had been made on the island hundreds of years ago and that it shouldn't be in a museum on the mainland, it belonged on Nantucket.

## A Haunted Theft

With a whoosh, freezing air engulfed Lin and she turned to see the Wampanoag ghost standing across the road. She faced him and this time, the sensation that filled her was not sadness and loss, but joy. The ghost held Lin's eyes for several seconds and he smiled at her. She nodded.

The front door opened and the ghost's atoms shimmered and swirled and he disappeared.

"Did your friend leave?" Jeff stepped onto the front stoop.

Lin looked at the handsome man standing in her front doorway. "She had to go."

Jeff smiled at Lin. "The tea's ready."

Lin walked over, walked up the steps, and stood in front of her boyfriend. She took his hand and said softly, "I've been wanting to talk to you about something."

Worry washed over Jeff's face.

"No worries." Lin put her hand softly against Jeff's cheek. "It's all good." She kissed him and the two walked into the house with their arms wrapped around each other.

It was time to stop keeping things from him. It was time to tell him about ghosts.

THANK YOU FOR READING!

BOOKS BY J.A. WHITING CAN BE FOUND HERE:

**www.amazon.com/author/jawhiting**

To hear about new books and book sales, please sign up for my mailing list at:

**www.jawhitingbooks.com**

Your email will never be sold, shared, or spammed.

# BOOKS BY J. A. WHITING

# LIN COFFIN COZY MYSTERIES

*A Haunted Murder* (A Lin Coffin Cozy Mystery Book 1)

*A Haunted Disappearance* (A Lin Coffin Cozy Mystery Book 2)

*The Haunted Bones* (A Lin Coffin Cozy Mystery Book 3)

*A Haunted Theft* (A Lin Coffin Cozy Mystery Book 4)

**And more to come!**

# SWEET COVE COZY MYSTERIES

*The Sweet Dreams Bake Shop* (Sweet Cove Cozy Mystery Book 1)

*Murder So Sweet* (Sweet Cove Cozy Mystery Book 2)

*Sweet Secrets* (Sweet Cove Cozy Mystery Book 3)

*Sweet Deceit* (Sweet Cove Cozy Mystery Book 4)

*Sweetness and Light* (Sweet Cove Cozy Mystery Book 5)

*Home Sweet Home* (Sweet Cove Cozy Mystery Book 6)

*Sweet Fire and Stone* (Sweet Cove Cozy Mystery Book 7)

**And more to come!**

J.A Whiting

# OLIVIA MILLER MYSTERIES

*The Killings* (Olivia Miller Mystery Book 1)
*Red Julie* (Olivia Miller Mystery Book 2)
*The Stone of Sadness* (Olivia Miller Mystery Book 3)

**If you enjoyed the book, please consider leaving a review.**

**A few words are all that's needed.**

**It would be very much appreciated.**

J.A Whiting

## ABOUT THE AUTHOR

J.A. Whiting lives with her family in New England. Whiting loves reading and writing mystery stories.

## VISIT ME AT:

**www.jawhitingbooks.com**

**www.facebook.com/jawhitingauthor**

**www.amazon.com/author/jawhiting**

Printed in Great Britain
by Amazon